The Legend Is Born

The Legends of Ḷainjin

Book Three

(Prequel to the Prequel)

The Legend Is Born

The Legends of Ḷainjin

Book Three

(Prequel to the Prequel)

A novel of historic literary fiction by Gerald R. Knight

Follow the history at GeraldRKnight.com

IGUANA

Published by Iguana Books
720 Bathurst Street, Suite 410
Toronto, ON M5S 2R4

Publisher: Meghan Behse
Editor: Shelley Egan
Cover designer: Jonathan Relph
Cover image by Herbert Kawainui Kane, with permission from Herbert K.Kane, LLC.
"Knowledge of the past gives us a rudder to navigate the present" — Herbert Kawainui Kane

ISBN 978-1-77180-586-5 (paperback)
ISBN 978-1-77180-585-8 (epub)

This is an original print edition of *The Legend Is Born: The Legends of Ḷainjin.*

The legend is born

He cried, seeming to say, "Where is she? You don't smell like her. You don't hold me the same way. I want my mother!" He was in a panic now and showed it with every wrinkle of his screaming red face.

His nervous but determined surrogate mother held a polished coconut shell full of boiled *jekaro*[1] and placed its eye to his mouth to see if he would suckle the sweet nourishing juice, but he was obviously having a tantrum. He kept turning his head and would have none of it. "I want my mother now!" he seemed to insist.

The young, bare-breasted woman bounced him gently in her arms and then swayed him from side to side, knowing he wanted the familiar smell he was used to. He wanted his mother to cuddle him close and wrap him in her warmth and peace. He turned his head from side to side as though searching through the blur for her. But the girl held him nonetheless and, despite his incessant crying, continued to hold him in her arms until he cried himself back to sleep. Then, after carefully wrapping him in the worn pandanus half skirt his mother had brought him in earlier that evening, his surrogate mother left him under the watch of her sister. The thatched house had been creaking from the force of the persistently growing storm, and Helkena was frightened and wanted to talk to her father. She climbed down the ladder through the single exit in the middle of the pole-house floor to the open space below.

---

[1] Also called "tuba," "toddy," and various other names; the sap of the coconut palm tapped from the flower bud as it grows and continues to protrude between its mature frond leaf and the less-mature inner fronds of the palm's inner crown. The skill of making jekaro is practiced worldwide, wherever palms grow.

The storm outside raged. Coconuts wrenched from the trees fell about the pebbled, leaf-strewn courtyard. The rain blew slanted through the open space under the house, forming puddles amid the thick pandanus matting that covered the beach stones spread beneath them. She hunched as she walked to the lee side of the home, where her father and the rest of the family had congregated to peer through the darkness at the bending coconut trunks with their nodding, rustling crowns. Leaves, and even limbs, had blown off the surrounding breadfruit trees. Luckily, there were no limbs above the house and no coconut trees next to it.

"Is this a typhoon, Father?"

"I think so."

"How's the boy?" her mother asked.

"Not good. He cried himself to sleep. Wouldn't drink his jekaro."

"He'll get used to it. They all do. It just takes one taste," she said.

Helkena spoke to her father again. "How did his mother know a typhoon was about to strike?"

"I saw her come back from the ocean side before she gave her command to set sail. She shouted, '*Emejjia wa iḷometo*!'[2] I heard her myself."

"But what did Tarmālu[3] see that alerted her?" Helkena was curious.

"The tide there must have told her something. It's the night of no moon, and you'd expect a high tide. But everyone this evening said they'd never seen a tide so high! It took the flotsam lining the shores up and over the strand."

"The high tide caused the typhoon?"

"No, of course not," her father said. "But maybe it's a characteristic. Listen to the waves falling there on the lagoon shore."

"They're very loud!"

"Yes, but the tide is low there now. And the waves pound hard even though the wind isn't coming from that direction. That tells me that, if the back side of this storm slaps us at high tide, the lagoon water might wash over the shore and flood the island," he said, worried.

That was an eventuality old people talked about around fires in the evening.

---

[2] "A boat dies slow in the open ocean."

[3] Ḷainjin's mother; Japeba's daughter.

He went on. "That same broad opening in the reef across the lagoon that allowed Tarmālu's fleet to escape the atoll will allow a west wind to whip *kāleptak* [4] into a giant swell. It will pour through the passage and break upon our lagoon beach. It might even suck our house into its backwash."

"*Jeej*![5] Where would we sleep then?"

"Let's hope the storm holds off a bit and comes ashore a little later tomorrow, once the tide is low again. That'll put more beach between our house and the shore. Better get back to the boy and hope for the best. But be prepared to tie yourself!"

Helkena went back up the ladder into the loft. She remembered the old people talking about tying themselves but had never thought such a thing would occur in her lifetime. It was cozy up here compared to the turbulence they faced below. The tightly folded thatch she and her mother had made, and that her father and the others had tied, kept the wind and rain outside. The window flaps that lined the house below the eaves and overlapped the walls were also tightly thatched. The simple wick of the coconut-shell lamp in the corner flickered, undisturbed.

"What did Father say? Are we going to die?" her sister, Jorkan, joked.

Helkena responded seriously. "Father says the wind will switch, come from the lagoon, whip up the waves, and threaten the village. But maybe it won't get that bad. I guess it depends on the timing of the storm and the tide." She glanced at the baby in her arms. "Look at him dreaming there peacefully, oblivious to all this."

The baby was content and at rest now, his face glowing in the lamplight.

"Well, he knows his mother is gone," replied Jorkan.

"He does, for sure, though he's not thinking of that now. But she wouldn't have left him here if she thought he was going to die. She was thinking about her boats and wanted them off that shore."

"Where will we go if…?"

---

[4] Swell that "slaps from behind"; the countercurrent of the Intertropical Convergence Zone, which periodically streams through the islands just north and south of the equator.

[5] An idiom used to express surprise. Translates roughly as "heck" or "darn it."

"Inland, I suppose. To the middle of the island. Maybe it's best you go below and get used to the storm like everyone else," Helkena suggested.

"Will I have to get wet?"

"No. Everyone is on the lagoon side, where it's still dry."

Jorkan went below, leaving them alone in the ever-creakier house. Her family had folded each pandanus leaf over a strip of coconut frond and threaded it with a coconut-leaf midrib that secured each leaf of the thatch shingles. Each shingle was the length of a man's arm. They had then tied and staggered these, one on top of the other, from ridge to eave.

The house stood on posts made of seasoned hardwood coconut trunks. The islanders had made the walls of the same materials as the roof, tied in the same way, and had lashed the thatch shingles to the poles that framed the structure. They had built these pole houses this way for ages, to be as flexible as their proas were on the ocean. The houses mimicked the proa's ability to rise and fall with the swells and to withstand the twisting force of the wind. Although their house still stood there, creaking but flexible, it would be no match against kāleptak swells pounding the shoreline if it came to that.

"The backwash could suck the sand and beach stones from around the posts, and the whole house could topple," Helkena thought, glancing at the house around her.

She laid her head next to her charge. His face was beautiful when it wasn't contorted and crying. There he was now, without a care in the world. "Ļainjin." She said his name out loud. Then she drifted into favorite thoughts about Tokki, a boy from Medyeron[6] she'd had her eye on. Not exactly a *rijeļā*,[7] that one, but there were so few boys her age she wasn't related to. She mulled over these favorite sentiments and drifted into a well-deserved nap.

Her sister awakened her a while later. Helkena was so tired she had no idea how much time had lapsed. All was surprisingly quiet now. The house no longer creaked, and that alone gave her spirits a lift, until her sister dropped her mood-changing words.

---

[6] An islet in the northwest corner of Wōtto Atoll.

[7] Literally, "bones that know"; traditional navigator; captain.

"Father says to bring the child below. He says it's time to tie ourselves!"

The words shocked her. They weren't what she had prepared herself for. She had expected to stay where she was until it all blew over, like so many times before. Then she remembered the stories of a lull before the strike. Was this what they had talked about?

She had lived on the shores of Wōtto,[8] the principal islet of this atoll, her whole life. With the predominant wind direction from the east, she had looked west, at the mostly peaceful lagoon, every day. The islet was so small she could walk its circumference in one morning. But it didn't seem small to her. At high tide, the surface of the lagoon rose right up to the beach's strand. The atoll was just a ring of flat coral islets, like a cup filled to its brim and ready to spill. But it didn't seem low in the water to her. Maybe, were she a bird that could fly high above and gain perspective, she might see things differently. She often tried to imagine that.

Hearing the lagoon waves thumping on the shore more clearly now that the weather had quieted, she knew what her father's words meant. The eye of the storm had passed over them, but its wind would come back from the opposite direction. This was their time to prepare, and she knew well from the stories what to do. She rolled her *jaki*[9] as tightly as possible. She grabbed her charge, with his mat wrappings, from where he lay and snuffed the lamp for safety's sake. Amid the blackness, holding the crying child in one arm, she found the exit and felt her way down the ladder. Her father was waiting and handed her the rope she was to use to tie herself. Now she was holding the boy, the jaki, and the rope.

"Do you want me to take the boy?" her father asked.

"No. Please, I've got him." His life would be in her hands, she thought.

"Okay, we'll head inland and find a thick coconut tree that's a little slanted and off by itself. The water will come from the lagoon, so we'll get to the middle of the island."

Her charge was crying again, but now Helkena was on a mission. She realized that everyone was abandoning the village. All the villagers were moving inland, and other children were crying. She wasn't alone. Her sister,

---

[8] Aka Wotho Atoll. "Wotho" is the contemporary spelling.

[9] Sleeping mat made of plaited pandanus leaves; "jaki ko" is the plural of "jaki."

father, mother, brothers… They moved as one group, as did the others. The rain had stopped, and she was glad for that. Looking up, she was surprised to see stars. To the unsuspecting eye, the storm was over. "Was this movement inland really necessary?" she wondered. She kept stumbling in the dark. There were so many broken limbs, and no real path to where they were heading.

Her father, always the leader, took his family to a spot he had in mind and started pointing out trees to each of them. He let her continue to hold the baby while he tied her to a tall coconut tree.

"Right over left," he said out loud, always teaching. "Left over right. Done." Then she saw him in the distance, tying himself to the same tree as her mother. "What was the sense of that?" she asked the baby in a singsong voice. "If she stays protected behind the tree, he'll be exposed to the weather!" Her mother, being her mother, must have insisted, and her brave, ever-suffering father had complied.

Ḷainjin hadn't stopped crying, so she lifted his face to hers and baby-talked to him in as carefree a voice as possible. He wasn't amused in the least and wanted his mother, but she had long since gathered her fleet, crossed the lagoon, sailed through the broad passageway, and got her craft safely to sea. Suddenly, it turned dark again as clouds covered the sky.

She remembered that first day well. Ḷainjin's mother, Tarmālu, fat with child, had brought hundreds ofbundles of *bwiro*[10] to trade for Wōtto logs of *jāānkun* and jaki.[11] Right off, she had asked for a midwife, and everybody pointed to Helkena's mother's house. So, that's how it started. She gave birth and, as the moons passed, the jaki and the *jāānkun* piled up as she distributed the bundles of *bwiro*. The *jāānkun* would supply nourishment during the trade-winds season when food was scarce, and the women of Wōtto made very fine jaki, and their men dried fine *jāānkun* as well. Sunlight they had in abundance.

So, the women of the island had gathered ever more pandanus leaves and made more mats. As Ḷainjin had grown, things slowed down. Helkena had

---

[10] Uncooked breadfruit that has been mashed and preserved. It is somewhat odorous.

[11] Sun-dried sheets of pandanus pulp rolled into a log and wrapped in a sheath of pandanus leaves. Taken for sustenance on long voyages.

helped her mother gather various leaves, which they heated with water in a *jāpe*[12] for Tarmālu's baths. Yesterday had been the second day of the storm, and then that evening, she decided to leave and off they went.

And here in Helkena's arms was Ḷainjin, the infant left behind. She held him between the tree and herself so she could brace him in her arms against the trunk. Peering into his little face and smiling, she said, "You're a heavy boy! Too much mother's milk." The storm, it seemed, was restarting, or at least clouding over again, and she was already tired of holding him. She looked over at her sister, who acknowledged her by raising her arm.

She remembered again what her father had said: "When the back side of this storm slaps." As if to emphasize that thought, a light breeze brushed her face, and just as her father had predicted, it came from the lagoon side this time.

Her mother had mentioned that Tarmālu had the *ṃōjọliñōr*.[13] "Too much sky inside," her mother had said. Tarmālu had been on the ocean too long. For her, land was just a resting place. Somewhere to stop on her endless journey back and forth among the atolls. She nearly always slept outside. Most people wanting air at least slept under the house, but she slept on her boat sometimes. Not a good sign. Maybe Tarmālu wasn't cut out to be a mother. In that case, she should have returned to her home island, where the boy could be adopted by a family member.

"Who wouldn't want such a beautiful boy?" Helkena baby-talked again. "He's a beautiful boy. Yes, he is."

When it started to drizzle, her first thought was to protect the baby. With some difficulty, she unrolled the jaki, folding it lengthwise because the rope that tied her limited its width to that of the tree. She slid the folded jaki up the trunk of the tree behind the boy and inside the rope that tied them. The jaki bent around them like a wall and bent over them, forming a roof of sorts. "That should help keep the rain off him," she thought, just as the wind picked up a little.

What a decision the boy's mother had made. But at this point, how could Helkena judge whether she was right or wrong?

---

[12] A wooden, trapezoid-shaped vessel carved from breadfruit wood and used as a cooking vessel or to knead breadfruit.

[13] Too much sky inside; sickness caused by sleeping under the moon too often.

"To Tarmālu, life was all about trading," she thought. On Wōtto, it was *bwiro* for *jāānkun* and jaki. Somewhere else, she heard it was something else for yet another product. But perceptively, Tarmālu would always take plenty of other things to give away — usually pandanus or breadfruit cuttings, mostly from the southern atolls to the northern ones. Her father had been ecstatic with the Ajbwirōk and Utōttōt varieties of pandanus cuttings she'd given him. He had planted them right off and watered them every day. Tarmālu had been to Wōtto several times. Being in the north, it was one of the drier islands, so perhaps she had felt it needed more of her help.

The people always welcomed her. This time, she had brought a full belly and asked Helkena's mother to help her give birth. Just like that. As though it was no big thing to bear a first child.

"And out popped Ļainjin," Helkena said out loud, kissing Ļainjin's forehead. "Your mother is a brave one. No doubt about that!"

Ļainjin looked at her as though trying to decide whether he should keep crying until his mother returned. She imagined him saying to himself, "Surely, she got my point by now! Mother must have gone away. Can mothers do that? Why did this woman take me from that warm place and bring me here?" He decided to keep crying.

Just then, a gust hit them with a swoosh of rain. Luckily, the tree and the folded mat protected them from most of it. Yet water started dripping from her face and seeping into the mat skirt he was swaddled in.

Tarmālu was a woman impossible to emulate. They all said that. With her cuttings and plantings, she had her eye on their future. Everyone could see that. She would show up one day on the horizon with twelve or so proas, which would tack across the lagoon. The village men would cut *pāp*[14] rollers and help them beach their proas. She'd meet with the elders and pass out her gifts to them from each boat. The elders were the first to hear the news she brought from the other atolls. Then she would meet with whomever would host her stay and present more gifts there. And almost always, she brought fish as well. The other boat *rijelā* and crew would meet with their hosts and distribute their gifts. Then, usually the next day, she

---

[14] The base of the coconut frond up to where the leaflets begin; coconut-leaf stems are often used as rollers to slide a boat up or down the shore.

would lay out her trade items beneath the house of her hosts and begin trading off the rest of what she had brought.

The wind was gusting now as it had before the lull, only from the opposite, more dangerous direction. Previously, the huge swells created by the fierce winds had crashed onto the broad ocean-side reef that protected the islet, but there was no reef protecting the lagoon side. Now, according to her father, it was just a matter of time before the wind built the swells rolling across the lagoon through the broad passageway on the other side to the point that they would crash over the lagoon beach and swamp the islet itself.

"How high will I be able to climb?" she wondered, looking up the trunk of the tree.

That juncture, she knew, would test her preservation skills to the limit. How much of this cold rain could she and the boy survive? Yes, the mat would help to shield them from the force of the wind, but she realized that the thick force of the constant rain would drench them and the wind would suck the heat from their bodies as they stood against it. "We'd be better off swimming," she thought. "At least the motion would heat us." This wasn't the warm rain of a cloud passing through an otherwise bright afternoon. Nor was it ocean water, which was warmer than the air of the storm. It was rain as cold as this typhoon could cough up, and it would leave them both shivering for their very lives.

Through the cold darkness, the rain soon began blowing in one gust after another. The tide rose as night progressed toward dawn. The high tide brought with it the swells that thumped onto the lagoon shore and swept inland. The water rose so high out of the ground surrounding them that Helkena had to climb the tree by placing the soles of her feet against the trunk and leaning back for support against the rope that tied them. All thoughts of the boy's mother, all thoughts of the previous days, all thoughts of everything but the present turmoil of the storm abandoned her now.

Strangely, the boy had long since stopped crying as he pressed tightly against the warmth of her body, seeming to accept the reality of the storm as too much to fight against. It dwarfed them both with its terror. She pressed his naked body against her bare bosom, covered him again with his mother's mat skirt, now sopping wet, and leaned back, supported by the rope. Her hair flying unbound behind her like the angry telltale feathers at the leech of his mother's sail, she closed her eyes and kept that posture as the seawater swamped the land below. Time passed drudgingly from one torturous moment to the next. Uprooted trees periodically punctuated the constant rush of the storm. Nearby coconut trees toppled with but a whimper against the pervasive howl of the wind. She looked not for her family at risk but rather, pressing the child tightly against her, simply chose to live for one more moment.

When the new day slowly arrived, she hardly noticed. She had kept her eyes closed to shut out the rain for so long she hardly dared to open them. The sun's path was deeply clouded. By mid-afternoon, the gusts began to lighten enough for her hair to fall back onto her shoulders, and she sensed that the worst of it was over.

After another while, her father waded over to them. "How is the boy?"

"He stopped crying. His heart still beats," she said, not wanting to separate Ḷainjin's naked body from hers to show her father and release the mutual heat.

"I'm going to see how the village fared." He began trudging shoreward through the swamped coconut and pandanus forest.

She lowered her feet into the quagmire below. The water came to her knees. Her back ached from resting against the rope that tied them to the tree. She stretched, still holding the baby close to her. All she could think about now was the warmth and comfort of the house they had left the night before. She hoped it would still be there and stood in the rain like that for a time, waiting impatiently for her father to come back. When he did return, he told her it was time to go back to the village. She asked him to hold the baby as she rolled the jaki again. Then she took him back and waded through the swamped islet. With no protection now against the rain and desperate for shelter of any kind, she didn't wait for the others in her family. As she walked, she suddenly felt pride she had survived. In a moment of levity, she wondered if she'd meet anyone along the way and chuckled. She must look like a half-drowned rat.

Then she arrived at the village, and disappointment quickly overcame all hope she'd had of returning to a dry, warm house. The sturdy pole houses had all collapsed, every one. House stilts lay abandoned in the sand on the shore, some still stuck in the ground with the houses they had once supported blown onto the courtyards behind them. It occurred to her there would be no shelter, no food, and certainly no water. Death from thirst or starvation invaded her thoughts, accompanied by the persistent rain and the constant pounding of the lagoon swells in the now-retreating tide. The only fortunate thing was that the village, after having had ocean-side beach stone spread there by hand for how many hundreds of seasons, stood on a higher, more porous base and hadn't been swamped.

Exhausted, she stooped beneath the peak of their collapsed and tattered home and hunched over the baby, waiting for the others in her family to arrive. The peak overhung the gable and offered some relief from the constant downpour. Still others had entered the village before her and were puttering around in equal dismay. Many homes seemed to have disappeared entirely, perhaps swept into the lagoon, as her father had warned.

She hugged the baby close to her breast with one hand and attacked the thatched gable of the toppled house behind her. With her free hand, she began tearing at the thatch below the peak of the roof. Once she had found the sennit cord that tied the thatch to the vertical poles, she was able to remove a row of shingles, and struggled on until she had removed a second row. Looking inside the dark, fallen hut, she saw the inside wall, which had collapsed on the ground beneath it. Next, she attacked the vertical pole that prevented her from entering, untying its lashings above and below so she could slide it aside. Now there was just enough room to squeeze under the roof at its peak. Lifting one leg and then the other, she backed into her sanctuary, carrying the boy. She sat on the collapsed thatched wall beneath her, which was surprisingly dry. It was now late afternoon, and this was the first time she had felt sheltered since the middle of the night before.

"Oh, what a relief to be out of that rain," she thought, now experiencing the luxury of thinking again rather than simply reacting to the weather that had inundated her. She held the baby tight against her bare bosom, feeling his beating heart and his warm body against her. When the others arrived, she stuck her head through the opening at the gable and asked her brother, who was standing there, to please find a coconut to husk for the child. Her mother, still standing in the rain outside, then asked for the skirt that had wrapped the boy. From beneath the thatch that extended beyond the gable, she thoroughly wrung the excess water out of the skirt. Helkena then hung it to dry by tucking its corner beneath the ridge pole. There was plenty of room left in her shelter, so she invited her mother and sister to join her. Her mother, being less agile, declined, but her sister quickly entered.

"That was the worst, the most tiring experience," said Jorkan, crawling into the corner where the roof was lowest to the ground. "I'm taking off these wet skirts, and I don't care who sees me lying here, naked as Ļainjin. I'm going to sleep for three days."

"Just think of the stories you'll be able to tell your grandchildren around the fire," commented their mother from outside.

"Grandchildren? I must have children first! Tokki is one of the few boys I'm not related to, and Helkena has her eye on him!"

"I do not!" Helkena said, defending herself.

Then her mother added her oft-spoken refrain. "Soon your father will arrange for you two to travel to Āne-pin̄[15] to get your lines, and you'll have your chance to bring back nice men."

How her brother managed to find a husking stake Helkena had no idea, but after a while, he returned with a ripe coconut that had perhaps fallen in the storm. When she offered the mouth of the husked nut to Ļainjin, he began sucking it at once. She was thrilled. This was the first liquid he had taken. Suddenly, their situation had turned from desperate to livable, and she didn't envy those still outside in the wind and rain.

Her father and younger brother occupied themselves with repairing the roof above them. Then her older brother came back with a round of coconuts for everyone. After drinking hers, Jorkan, exhausted, keeled over on her side and fell asleep at once.

When the boy had had enough to drink, Helkena finished the coconut and broke it open. She scooped out a thumbnail of the immature, custard-like nut and put it in his mouth. Now, with time to think, she tried to remember exactly when he had stopped crying. At some point during the night and the following morning, he must have realized the futility of

[15] An islet of Aelōn̄ļapļap famous for its tattooing traditions.

complaining and simply accepted the situation for what it was. He looked up at her now, and she imagined he was thankful for the water and the food and her continued protection. After he had eaten his fill, she ravenously finished the coconut herself then lay on her side, snuggling the baby tight and following her sister into a deep, relaxing sleep.

The pouring rain persisted though the wind continued to taper. At high tide, the swells breached the shore once again, but not the village, where the land was higher.

It was still raining early the next morning, when she left her sleeping charge with her sister and got up to urinate. She was happy to see that her father, mother, and brothers had made a lean-to from another collapsed thatch wall to protect themselves against the weather and were sleeping comfortably. It rained all the next day. Again, her brother brought them coconuts. The heat from their sleeping bodies dried the boy's wrap, and he snuggled within it again. He continued drinking and eating. Finally, on the fifth day after the start of the storm, the rain stopped. That evening, a well-formed new moon appeared in the western sky at sunset. That night, the clouds began to pass, and the village seemed to awake to a fresh day.

The men of the village went from house to house, repairing roofs and walls where they stood, and the women gathered pandanus leaves inland to process for the reconstruction to come. A few walked the reefs west and south to gather news of how their sister islets had fared in the storm. No doubt not as badly. Those islets were at the corners of the triangular-shaped atoll, sheltered by reefs and not in the direct path of the kāleptak swell. Then the women hung their jaki ko to dry in the tailwinds of the storm and brought baskets of stones, newly washed up by the typhoon, to cover the sandy floors of the makeshift structures so there was proper shelter for all. Some of the men went to work repairing the several small fishing canoes and proas that, surprisingly, had survived the storm. These boats had washed inland off the strand, where they had sat protected in their boathouses. Most had their outriggers broken in one place or another, and some had crashed into trees. But the islanders needed to fish and wanted to visit the other two inhabited islets. So, they dismantled the craft, carried them back to shore, and reconstructed them there.

The young men tried their luck at pole fishing and brought back small fish that the people divided up and ate raw. With all the dampness, no one had yet managed to start a fire. But things were drying out, and the sun showed through the clouds the next day, restoring more hope among the people that life would eventually return to normal. The day after, someone did manage to start a fire, and they were on their way. Their problem, of course, was water.

The islet had a narrow, freshwater lens that floated on top of the saltwater within the islet's sandy base, an arm's length or so beneath the ground. The level of this water rose and fell with the tides. The typhoon had dumped a great deal of freshwater on the island to be sure. However, the ocean water had crept over the shore and then polluted it. They could bathe in the brackish water, but it was no good for drinking, and it would take time for the two to naturally separate. The islanders had coconuts, but one tree produces only one bunch of coconuts per cycle of the moon. They had to be careful not to consume them all before their freshwater lens could restore itself.

The men took to the trees to produce jekaro. It was the sweet juice that seeped from a freshly cut bud of the coconut tree, but not all trees were good for jekaro. Helkena's brothers had had several trees going before the storm and tried to revive them after with some luck. She was quick to appropriate for the baby a little of what they'd brought down in netted coconut shells. He drank it this time and quickly developed a taste for it. Jekaro hosted a natural yeast that grew on the bud. By noon, the yeast would turn the jekaro from clear to milky, and its nutritional value grew with the yeast. However, the liquid needed to be heated to kill the yeast by late afternoon, or it would turn alcoholic.

Soon a few of the canoes came into repair. The men took them fishing, and the women cooked the fish, and the nourishment sustained them. Helkena fed Ļainjin mashed fish and washed it down with jekaro. Occasionally, a proa would arrive from the atoll's southeast or southwest to view the destruction they themselves had missed. Probably, her father explained, because the islets of their atolls hadn't faced the built-up slap of kāleptak the way their islet had, or because they were out of the typhoon's haphazard path. They lent their hands but, not wanting to be a burden on the water supply, left as quickly as they had come. As the days passed, several families walked the reef of the atoll to move in with family, mostly west to Medyeron but some to Kabben,[16] to the south. Both islets had plenty of water in their wells, but water became the biggest obstacle to life on Wōtto. By the middle of the next moon following the typhoon, all progress in the village stopped due to a lack of drinking nuts. Their father began talking about walking the reef themselves. Their islet needed more time to recover its habitability.

The intrepid old warrior called Japeba[17] and his brother arrived on the next new moon through the broad gap in the reef on the western horizon, in a large proa with an unusual J-shaped curve in the *rojakkōrā*[18] of its sail. The auburn rays of the setting sun clearly illuminated the sail's silhouette as it headed for Medyeron, at the northwest edge of the atoll. That night, the islanders saw strange fires on the beach there, and the next morning, the proa left Medyeron and sailed, as though on a mission, straight toward them.

The whole village quickly grew alert to the arrival of this strange proa. It sailed low in the calm blue water as though weighted down with something. Helkena, curious girl that she was, stood with the baby on the beach as it landed. It had a short, fat *kubaak*,[19] and its sail had an odd shape. The two elder men sailing the canoe, who resembled each other and had a casual, friendly manner, had managed the large proa with a high degree of poise and efficiency. They were hardened men of the sea with no wasted motion to their actions — everyone could see that. The oarsman had a serious face; the other, tending the sheet, an engaging smile. Their long hair wasn't tied up in a bun in the style of Rālik[20] men. They had simply tied it in the back as a man at work would do. They wore not fine kilts of pandanus and hibiscus fiber but everyday *in*[21] made of *atat*,[22] with fibers in front and back, fastened by a band that left their thighs darkened by the sun. They were obviously from islands

[16] The southernmost islet of Wōtto Atoll.

[17] Jipeba's older brother; Tarmālu's father.

[18] Literally, "spar woman"; the lateral boom of the triangular lateen sail.

[19] Outrigger float.

[20] The western chain of atolls of what is now known as the Republic of the Marshall Islands.

[21] Skirt or kilt made of various fibers other than grass.

[22] A plant with small, thin leaves; the stems of this plant, *Triumfetta procumbens*, were processed to make skirts or kilts.

to the west but appeared as everyday sailors, not as dignitaries. Their mission — to help with the islanders' plight — became clear almost at once.

The two men had emptied the contents of their vessel and filled their hull from freshwater wells at Medyeron. After the men of the village helped them beach their heavy proa, the two dug a hollow in the sand beneath and announced to all that they were welcome to bring their netted water shells and fill them. Their hull had a hole drilled through the bottom that was plugged from the inside. They normally used this to drain any seawater once the canoe was beached. Instead, they had plugged this hole from outside of the hull, allowing them to fill all the netted coconut water shells the people brought. Something about these kind men intrigued Helkena. They were men of the west but spoke fluent Kajin Rālik.[23] After hearing about their plight, they had sailed all the way from Naṃdik[24] to help.

The somewhat younger of the two westerners noticed Helkena there, holding the child, and approached her. She had never seen a man with such a kind twinkle in his eyes, and he put her at ease. His face was sun darkened and wrinkled, and his tattoos were not from Rālik. The baby was unwrapped, so the man could see it was a boy.

"What's his name?"

"Ḷainjin," she said proudly.

"Whose child is he?" Undoubtedly, he had noticed her unsuckled breasts.

"He belongs to Tarmālu. I'm just caring for him until she returns."

"What are you feeding him?"

"What else? Jekaro and fish!"

"And you're doing a wonderful job. I can see that. He looks happy and contented."

Helkena was surprised he didn't ask about Tarmālu. But she was from Naṃdik too. Perhaps he had already heard.

That evening, having unloaded their cargo of water from Medyeron, the men crossed the lagoon in their swift canoe in short order and trolled for tuna along the sunken western reefs. They strapped the tunas across their

---

[23] Language of the Rālik Islands, now the western chain of the Republic of the Marshall Islands.

[24] Aka Namorik. Where Ḷainjin lives; part of the Rālik string of islands.

large outrigger platform and returned to feed the whole island. The next morning, they did the same, and the next evening, they fished a third time and took their fish and spent that night at Medyeron.

House reconstruction soon resumed, now that these men had solved their sustenance problem. The days seemed to pass more quickly now, and there was so much for the villagers to do. Pandanus leaves to gather and process. Thatch poles to cut. The westerners continued their back-and-forth between the islets of the atoll. The two had taken a liking to Ļainjin and never failed to stop by to say hello when they returned. They brought treats of bananas and coconuts from Medyeron, and the boy recognized and remembered them. They held him high in the air and made him giggle. All the while, the water in the island wells became sweeter. The heavier saltwater from the flooding finally filtered through the fresh water that floated on top of it. The next two moons seemed to pass just as quickly. Soon the trade winds would arrive, and before then it would be time for the brothers to return to Naṃdik.

One day, Helkena was sitting with the boy under her favorite *kiden*[25] tree, looking out over the peaceful lagoon, when the westerners approached her. Since her youth, it had been her favorite spot to look at the beautiful azure colors and appreciate her home on the edge of the sea. Moreso now that her only chore was to look after the boy, who had long since learned to roll over and seemed ready to crawl. As was their wont, the men began holding him up in the air and putting their sun-darkened faces up to his to make him laugh. Then they asked, Were her mother and father available to speak. She left the boy with them and found her father and mother, still repairing thatch shingles on the side of their makeshift house.

"Come, the two westerners want to speak with you." Helkena sensed this was something important. Her parents had only rarely spoken to the two before.

The younger man spoke first. "This is my brother. His name is Japeba. My name is Jipeba.[26] Have you heard where we are from?"

Yes, they had heard that the westerners sailed all the way from Naṃdik

---

[25] Soldierbush: *Tournefortia argentea.*

[26] Japeba's younger brother.

to help.

Then they got to their proposal. Did they know that Tarmālu was Japeba's daughter?

This was a possibility no one had mentioned, but all knew that Tarmālu had been raised on Naṃdik. Some had perhaps assumed these two had come looking for her, but this knowledge came as a complete surprise to Helkena.

Jipeba explained that Japeba, her father, was the one who had taught her how to read the tides and the clouds. He was the one who had taught her how to sail, and, with their permission, they hoped to do the same for the boy. Would Helkena consider leaving Wōtto for Naṃdik with them, to help them raise the lad? They went on about the details of the trip, but she didn't listen to anything after that. Her mother had questions, and so did her father, but she was shocked and lost in thought. They must have realized this and stopped talking. They just sat there and played with the boy to give her time to consider their proposal.

Had Tarmālu's fleet of proas managed to sail but a short distance from the atoll and then taken down their sails, leaned to, and drifted in the storm, surely, they would have been back by now. How far could they have drifted in three or four days? Helkena had no idea. What other eventuality might have occurred she couldn't even guess. Now that she forced herself to think it through, she realized how much time had passed. Was it possible the fleet had gotten lost in the storm? But wasn't Tarmālu famous for never losing her way out there? Their ancestors had passed down the expression "Emejjia wa iloṃeto." Upon her fleet's departure, she had said this herself. What happened to them, and would she ever return for the boy? What if Tarmālu did return? Didn't Ḷainjin now consider her his mother? Surely, she would still be needed for a period.

These thoughts now poured through her mind like the storm that had bound them together. These kind men only wanted what was best for their grandson. Their words "with your permission" hung in her thoughts. Who was she to give permission? Tarmālu had left the boy with her mother. It was a twisted situation. Helkena had never sailed into the ocean on a proa before. No opportunity had presented itself. Was she afraid? Of course, now more than ever… But yes, she was ready to go with them. A lot of men lived on

Naṃdik, and none of them would be relatives!

She looked at her parents from afar now, having long since closed her ears to their conversation. Sitting there, the two of them were basically negotiating. What was her mother to do without her? She was her eldest daughter. Her father was looking for more pandanus cuttings when they returned. She didn't have the throat to tell them she wasn't likely to return for seasons and would likely have a family by then. Tarmālu was probably dead. These kindly men knew it. Suddenly, she realized how small her parents' world really was. Yes, they knew this small world well. They were skilled and she would miss them, but their horizon limited their view. Now seeing this for the first time, she looked out over her precious lagoon as if for the last time. "Yes, every woman's horizon is limited, but sailing over that horizon and seeing for myself what is past it — even if only ocean — might make all the difference," she thought. That perspective was calling to her.

"When do we leave?" she asked, ending whatever negotiations were taking place.

"Not for several days. We'll give you time to talk it over."

"Okay," she said, with a decisive nod of her head and a smile. Shortly, the two men left the family there beneath the *kiden* tree. They wandered off into the village, perhaps quitting the conversation while they were ahead.

Her mother chastised her. "Why so soon to agree?"

"He's got their blood. What can I say? We can't just hand him over now. After all Ḷainjin has been through, I can't do that to him. The two elders are right in asking me to go with them. He must be handed over to them very gradually. Besides, this is the only place I've ever known, and suddenly, it looks surprisingly small."

"Looks to me like she caught the 'goes' from them, and when a woman gets the 'goes,' she's gone, and there's nothing anyone can do about it," said her father.

"Well, I guess all is said. Just bring back a nice man from there to work our land," her mother added, completing their agreement.

"Oh, I will. You can be certain about that!"

When Helkena went to her spot in the shade of the *kiden* tree the next morning, Jipeba — the younger of the western visitors — was there. Sitting off to the side with his adze, he was hacking at an old block of breadfruit wood.

"What are you making?" she asked casually. She deftly unfolded her jaki with one hand while holding the boy with the other.

"I'm making a *lem*[27] with an extra-long handle for you to scoop water up into your little house from the sea."

"Little house?"

"Yes, my brother is over there building a little shelter for you on the outrigger platform of our proa. It will give you a dry place to rest and offer privacy for your needs. There will be enough space between the *apet*[28] so you can reach down and scoop up seawater with this *lem* to wash the boy when he eliminates."

"Oh, I was wondering about that just last night!" She realized Jipeba was talking about the boy, but the information pertained to her too. Now that she thought about it, the house would provide privacy for the men as well.

"Another thing I was worried about… What if we get caught in another storm in the middle of our trip? I've never been anywhere before."

"That's easy to answer," Jipeba said. "My brother knows how to predict weather. He watches the colors in the sky every morning and evening. We're going to take as good care of you as we would our own daughter. We'll do everything we can to make sure your trip to Naṃdik and back is as tolerable as possible. And please don't think we plan to make a servant of you. We're crusty old bachelors. We take care of everything ourselves. That boy is used to your arms, and continuing to take care of him is all we expect from you. Plan to get fat and happy!" With that, he turned away from his hacking and looked at her with an endearing glance that only a man telling the absolute truth could give.

"I can hardly wait! I hear there are plenty of eligible men on Naṃdik."

"Trust me, they'll make pests of themselves! You'll have the pick of

---

[27] A wooden scoop, sometimes attached to a handle, used to bail water from a hull or retrieve water from the ocean.

[28] The two spars that curve downward and attach the outrigger float, or "kubaak," to the underside of the outrigger platform.

them."

"Oh, I'm not picky. Just looking for a good man willing to come here and work our mother's lands."

"We'll have to get you your lines first," suggested Jipeba. "Would you like that?"

"Oh, yes. I'd given up on Āne-pin̄ and was planning on having a woman do them."

"Well, there's a woman on Naṃdik. Her name is Lijitwa, and she was a renowned tattooist at Āne-pin̄ for many seasons. We'll ask her to do it. We'd be honored to sponsor your lines."

"Thank you. That would be a plan completed!"

"The men of Naṃdik are like men everywhere," Jipeba said. "Just looking for a good piece of land to supply security for their daughters and a place to raise their sons. The boys, on the other hand, are just looking for… Well, you know."

"Oh yes, I know. Some girls are like that too, and then they end up with a boy father for their child and wonder why they're thirsty for coconut water and hungry for fish. A boy must show he's a man before I'll even consider him."

"With that attitude, you'll do fine. I could name several men right now, but better for you to make your own decision."

Helkena was excited at this prospect and sat there, naturally apprehensive about the trip but quite satisfied with her bargain.

Jipeba spent the rest of the morning and part of the afternoon carving out the oblong, scoop-shaped bailer and lashing it to the *kiden* pole he had cut for it. Of course, there was other chitchat, but the substance of their agreement had concluded.

After a few more days, the weather turned solidly back to the east, and there was a new moon again. All knew the trade winds were about to begin and the window for open-ocean sailing was about to close. The people of Wōtto gave them a remarkable send-off. The singing, dancing, and food sharing lasted the whole evening before. The parting gifts were plentiful and delayed their departure from dawn to midmorning.

Helkena's mother brought an elaborately plaited face mat that she would wear while being tattooed. "Remember, a woman knows pain! We don't cry out in childbirth, and we certainly don't cry out when they tap us with their *ñi.*"[29]

"Bring back a good one!" were her sister's parting words.

Finally, by midmorning, they were off. The small hut they had constructed on the outrigger platform was large enough to store all the gifts and left enough room for Helkena to lie inside. But she wasn't ready for that. She sat outside the little door of the hut, holding her charge tight to her body as they crossed the lagoon's smooth waters, the sun blazing hot on her fair skin. She watched the big plaited-pandanus sail pop with air as they sailed from the island's lee shores and crossed the lagoon, surprised at how rapidly her island shrank in size. The wind propelled them forward with what she perceived as incredible speed. When they got to the sunken reefs below the broad passage to the ocean, she marveled at the multicolored corals below.

Their craft began to rise and fall in the smooth kāleptak swells that crossed the lagoon and washed up on the shores of the islet they had just left. It was less than the length of her fingertip above the eastern horizon now. It was but a spot of white beach below a cap of greenish-brown at the end of a necklace of other much smaller islets that lined the eastern horizon all the way down to Kabben. She had walked that reef to her right a few times and had canoed there also. She had walked the reef now behind her on her left to Medyeron as well. But with her horizon now expanding, she began to realize what their conversation of the days before had only hinted at. The world was certainly a bigger place than she had always imagined. And suddenly, the thought that their destination was far out there beyond that distant horizon frightened her. Why had she agreed to undertake such a long journey?

The younger of the elders, the talkative Jipeba, manned the sheet from a lee platform that was less than a quarter the size of the windward platform that she sat on. Perhaps sensing her thoughts from her wide and wandering eyes, he said, "It's an ocean world out there, scattered with islands big and small."

From the stern hull and manning the oar, Japeba spoke his first words. "Wōtto has a lagoon shaped like a banana that's fat at the north end. It has a

---

[29] Tattooing chisel made of albatross bone; the sharp teeth of this tool.

larger lagoon than Naṃdik. But Naṃdik is a much larger island that almost extends around the whole atoll. It has a round lagoon with two landless reefs leading to a second islet called Marmar.[30] There is no true passage between ocean and lagoon along those reefs. No direct way to enter or exit the atoll. You'll see."

"But it's so far away! When will we get there?" she asked.

"With this wind, and these seas" — Japeba looked out across the horizon — "it should take only a couple of days."

"A couple of days. No wonder they made the effort to construct this cute little house for us," she thought, looking back and clutching Ḷainjin more securely. She was having second thoughts, but it was too late now. Their bow was starting to gently tip as the swell her father called kāleptak rolled beneath them from the west.

As they headed south but three islets were ahead on the west side of the atoll, separated by two stretches of open reef before Kabben. Across the lagoon on the eastern side of the atoll, she counted eleven islets along a contiguous reef from Wōtto to Kabben, which marked the atoll's southern tip.

"You can stay out here until we pass the tip of the atoll. So far, the reefs have blocked the swell rolling from the east," said Jipeba. "Once we pass Kabben, you'll want to get the boy under cover. We're about to face *buñtokrear*,[31] the swell falling from the east. When we do, it will start to get rough, with *wa tutu*[32] blowing at us as its crest crashes into our *kubaak*."

Helkena decided to stay put if she could, but once they had passed the tip of Kabben, the unobstructed swell coming from the eastern direction quickly overcame its counterswell, kāleptak. The ocean churned more abruptly, the *kubaak* plunged more deeply into the oncoming swells, and the resulting spray released as the float rose from the sea began showering them with its spume. The little hut behind her afforded some protection from the spray, but its roof had no peak. Instead, it slanted up from the *apet* to which it was secured and rose only slightly higher than a seated person. So, the spray blew over its roof and drenched the other side. After a short while, the

---

[30] The northernmost islet of Namorik Atoll.

[31] Swell that "falls from the east."

[32] Boat spray; windblown ocean spray.

saltwater spray started dripping off her hair into the boy's happy, excited face. Clearly, this was the start of something unanticipated.

She tied her hair in a bun and withdrew into her little house, leaving the door open. She sat the boy up in her lap, her hands beneath his arms. There, he could look out at Jipeba manning the sheet from the leeward platform. Directly across from them, the platform angled skyward over the ocean. Already inundated in spray, the brothers were busy steering their prow over the crest of each crossing swell and down into the following trough, much as the way Jipeba liked to lift up the boy and then lower him down before raising him up again. As he always did, Ḷainjin watched the grizzly old salt Jipeba crack the smile that made him laugh — even more so now that the elder's face was dripping with sea water. Jipeba made a challenging chore look fun.

A pandanus mat covered the outrigger platform, which extended out toward the *kubaak* but ended at the last spar crossing the *apet*. Then there was the open space for her to draw water with the *lem* they had made for her. Did they expect her to squat there to go? When she looked back at the crusty mariner through the wind and spray, he seemed to have read her thoughts.

"Don't worry!" he shouted through the wind and spray. "This is the worst of it! By sunset, we should reach the shadow of Kuwajleen.[33] That atoll east of us will absorb the force of buñtokrear, and the sea will calm."

When she pulled the boy back into her arms, he was smiling again. "He seems to respond positively to the sea. Must be in his blood," Helkena thought. She was starting to get a little nauseated but thought it best to take care of his needs first. Picking him up, she crawled him windward and then held him under his arms, and over the opening beneath the little windward wall. Sure enough, his training came through, and he piddled where he was supposed to. For weeks now, she had been training him like that by squeezing his ding-a-ling when she caught him urinating and then holding him like that where she wanted him to go.

Helkena crawled him back to their spot on the mat, feeling quite dizzy now. In cheerful baby talk, she said, "Don't worry. Just wait until sunset, and things will get better." She turned on her side, tucked her legs, and lifted the

---

[33] Aka Kwajalein Atoll; islets of. The largest atoll in the Rālik Chain.

boy's head onto her arm. "Just wait," she repeated, as another bout of nausea gripped her. Closing her eyes, she suddenly felt sleepy and thought about taking a nap. Jipeba closed the door, and then they were alone in the dim light reflecting off the blue sea below the opening to windward. Nausea had gripped her but not the boy, who was as active as ever. He pumped his legs and waved his arms and looked around, studying the thatch ceiling of this unique abode. Obviously, he felt at home on the ocean, but she, not so. Leaving him there alone, she crawled rapidly back to windward and regurgitated the contents of her stomach into the froth below. Holding him steady with her foot, she coughed and spit into the sea, and after she returned to him, he studied her face as if to ask what was wrong. Then she curled up on her side with her arm around him, closed her eyes, and tried to sleep, wondering again why she had so quickly agreed to such a challenging trip.

Sleep, of course, wouldn't come. The craft twisted off the crest of each swell, plunged at a steep angle down its side, then righted abruptly as the swell passed, only to climb the next in monotonous repetition. Several more times, she scrambled to windward to look down into the white foam-crusted blue until no more liquid came forth from her stomach and her heaves turned dry. Each time, the boy smiled at her and took more cooked jekaro from the eye of the polished coconut shell. It had passed down from one generation of her family to another and had taken countless trips to the beach — filled each time with small coral pebbles, shaken with salt water, rinsed, shaken again, rinsed again until clean, then filled once more with the sweet, nourishing nectar.

Helkena remembered her mother's warning: a mother's tasks continue on past the sleep of others. "But how are those two outside to sleep?" she wondered. "Better in here than out there."

She curled up and struggled to sleep in the cozy but confining structure. But sleep came slowly if at all. With nothing to hold on to, she kept sliding as the boat heeled off the crest of each swell then tipped downward into its trough. So, she maneuvered herself to the hull side of the platform and wedged her feet against the sturdy hut frame lashed there. Then she braced her back against the hut's stern wall, also well framed and lashed down. With her left arm, she cradled the boy. And with her palm pressed firmly against the floor, she was able to prevent the two of them from sliding forward as the boat abruptly responded to whatever pitch the sea provoked. Although this rotation of stress from feet to back to palm kept her mind and body awake, it didn't relieve the nausea that sickened her.

The boy, on the other hand, seemed to thrive on the constant motion. He was used to being held, moved, and carried. Helkena not so, and she had never felt misery like this. Thus, her afternoon passed ever so slowly, but as the sun set, just as the salty one had predicted, the swell from the east slowly, imperceptibly, began to moderate. The swells became less steep. She had to brace herself less often. Her nausea lessened. She carried the boy windward for one final pee. Then she laid him down, cradled him next to her, and finally slept.

At dawn the next day, she awakened to more harsh seas like those of the day before, but somehow, her body had adapted during the night. The child was awake and crying for food, but first she crawled him windward. Curiously, he stopped crying. "Does he cry now to let me know he needs to urinate?" she wondered. Crawling back to the lee side, she opened the door so the smart boy could look out at the sparkling, rolling seas again.

"Any food out there?" Helkena asked, putting on the bravest face she could as she stuck her head out. The older brother, Japeba, was still at the helm. "Have you been there this whole time?"

"No, we relieve each other every quarter day and night. He's sleeping below, and it's time for our morning meal. You missed supper!"

"Yes, well, I wasn't feeling good. I couldn't keep down what I'd eaten."

"I understand. What about the boy?"

"He's fine." She held him up to look at the rolling, white-capped ocean.

"It's starting to get rough again, so we must be passing south of Kuwajleen," Japeba proclaimed, raising his chin and pointing his nose east.

Just then, his brother popped up out of the stern hold with an *anrā*[34] of fish and *jāānkun* and two coconuts.

"Oh, Ļainjin will love this." Instinctively, she smelled the day-old cooked fish to make sure it was still good. When she mashed a piece with her fingers and fed it to him, he gobbled it up, and she followed that with a sticky piece of jāānkun, which he ate as well. After feeding the boy, she ate a little herself

[34] A small tray made of coconut leaflets.

and washed it down with some coconut water. Her stomach still ached from all the retching the day before. The ocean was starting to get rough, and she didn't want to risk getting sick again.

"Well, back to my shell," she said, with as much humor as she could muster.

"That's a good place for you. Only one more day now," Japeba assured her.

When she closed the door, they were alone again in their flying house. The boy was smiling after his meal. It was a wonder how well he had taken to the ocean. Although she, too, felt more accustomed to it, she still had rest to catch up on, so they slowly fell back to sleep together. The realization that the ocean was an even bigger place than she had imagined came as she was falling asleep. It was unending. Could she truly trust these two to get them safely to Naṃdik and back? She hadn't imagined it was so far away, with so much ocean in between. But then, they hadn't given any reason to doubt their skills.

It was afternoon before she woke up to take the boy to pee, and she had postponed her own needs long enough. So, she turned around and balanced herself over the opening as best she could, given the rocking seas. The relief she felt made her wonder why she had held it so long. Then she opened the door again. Jipeba — the younger, more talkative brother — was at the helm. She fed the boy more fish and jāānkun from the *anrā*, and he ate it hungrily, as before. "Sooner or later, he's going to have to expel this stuff," she commented.

Jipeba laughed. "Your system has a way of tightening up at sea."

She looked out over the ocean. "All this water. Where does it end?"

"You can sail for moon upon moon and eventually, unbelievably, end up where you started, only coming from the opposite direction. The world is round just like the moon."

"Have you sailed around the world?"

"No, of course not. A man is but a stick worm in the forest. His life is too short to see it all."

"Are we on course to see Naṃdik tomorrow?"

"We will see Naṃdik tomorrow."

"Well, this stick worm is ready to crawl inside and take another nap."

"Come out again when it's time to eat. No one likes to eat alone."

She didn't open the door until that evening. The sun set in a red sky that foretold of fair weather, and that gave her the confidence she would need for the night ahead. They were now westward of the other atolls in the Rālik necklace. Japeba, the elder of the two, was on shift and warned her that the sea would get rougher as they traveled south. That was about all she got from the taciturn one. He was a kind man but never had much to say. "He's like a clam," she thought. "Happy inside his shell. As I get to know him better, he might open a little."

She tried to sleep again, but perhaps she had slept her fill. And with all the rocking now, she found it difficult to position herself. The boy was restless, too, and cried often to pee and something else. For the first time, she drew water from the sea with the *lem* Jipeba had made for her, although it was awkward to use it properly and hold Ļainjin.

Sometime in the middle of the night, she heard one of the two sing out, "*Jeļatae.*"[35] Then before dawn, the voice cried out, "*Dibukae.*"[36] At dawn, she heard "*Juae.*"[37] Were these markers of some sort, and did it mean they were close to Naṃdik?

She opened the door to her hut. The answer was yes. These distinct currents surrounded the atoll. The old mariner claimed he felt the island's presence in a swell called *buñtokiōñ*,[38] which fell from the north. He spent quite a bit of time trying to point it out to her, but its presence was too subtle for her to detect. Apparently, the swell from the north was getting more predominant because the atoll was progressively smothering its counterswell, *buñtokrōk*.[39] The swell from the east was still dominant, however, and that was all she could see and feel.

After a while, the younger of the brothers cried out that he'd spotted the island through the before-dawn darkness. She couldn't detect that sighting either but took his word for it and, satisfied they were on course, closed the door again and tried to nap. This time she awoke to Jipeba's

---

[35] An outer current surrounding an atoll

[36] An intermediate current surrounding an atoll.

[37] The innermost current surrounding an islet.

[38] Swell that "falls from the north."

[39] Swell that "falls from the south."

chanting as he hauled in a large tuna. In the early morning light, she opened the door in time to watch him club it and tie it to the leeward platform on which he had been sitting. He quickly tossed his lure back into the ocean, gradually untangling and then surrendering his twisted coir fiber line as the lure pulled it into the sea. But before he did, he kissed the large, heavy hook — painstakingly ground from *kapwōr*[40] shell — before releasing it into the blue water and chanting something. Flocks of birds were swirling about and diving into the water close by. She looked ahead and there, amid the dawn, was the green island of their destination, somewhat obstructed by salt yet clearly visible. She felt joyful. This trying voyage was almost over.

[40] Giant clam: Tridacna gigas.

The arrival

This was her first glimpse of another atoll, and truthfully, it was still a little too far away to tell if it looked anything like hers. Although they were making steady progress toward the atoll, Jipeba kept catching tuna, and that caused repeated delays. By midmorning, they were so close that Helkena could see the ring of land encompassing the entrance-less lagoon that Japeba had drawn for her. Then, as they sailed to lee of the single north-most islet, she spotted the huge stone landmarks on the western reef. That reef was one of two reefs on either side, separating the distant islet from the main, claw-shaped Naṃdik, which wrapped around the lagoon from one end to the other.

"There are no large stones scattered like that on the reefs of Wōtto," she thought. "Who could have rolled such stones up onto the reef like that?" The largest was bigger than a full-sized house.

Jipeba had finished fishing and was now coiling his trolling line on its spool. He had slid onto the forward deck from his perch on the leeward platform. Where he had been sitting, there was now room to line up and tie his catch of five various-sized tuna. Sitting cramped against the mast with his legs bent over one of the two *apet*, he was very close to Helkena now, though facing forward, away from her.

"A typhoon can be a very disruptive thing." Jipeba looked out over the reef before them. "That stone is called Diaj,[41] and legend says it was sitting there with the rest of them when our people first came here. Undoubtedly, they were broken from the reef by some horrendous storm that would have made the one that hit your island look like an evening shower."

[41] Immense coral rock on Namorik reef.

"I wouldn't want to have to live through that."

"Trust me, you wouldn't have!" said Jipeba. He turned his head half back toward her and nodded to show reverence for the power of the sea.

"Everything is so green!" she said.

"Wōtto is very dry, and its leaves are brown most of the year," he said. "Naṃdik gets a lot of rain. We have much breadfruit and freshwater taro swamps and many flavors of pandanus that the weather on Wōtto won't support."

"If there's no passage from the ocean, how do you get your boat into the lagoon?"

"We seldom take our proa into the lagoon. When we do, we just sail it over the reef at high tide. We normally surf proas over the reef edge and leave them on the ocean-side shore."

"Surf?" she asked.

"You'll see soon enough," Jipeba said, sneaking a glance at his brother. Japeba cracked a rare smile in response.

They were approaching the atoll at low tide along its western reef. Its eastern reef and the whole eastern side of the long, claw-shaped island were blocking the buñtokrear swell, so the sea was smooth now. They were sailing close to the reef, and kāleptak was rolling up against it along the way, emitting a sucking sound with its backwash, as though the reef was breathing in and out. When Jipeba pointed down into the sea below them, Helkena peered around the corner of the open doorway to see a dolphin swimming next to them. That was when she noticed all the canoes fishing in the open sea ahead of them.

"*Drej lotipen*!"[42] exclaimed Jipeba.

She knew the fishing term well. On occasion, her father would cross the lagoon in his canoe, enter the ocean through the passage, and drift there in the open ocean, fishing for tuna with a longline. Here, fishermen just had to cross the reef and they were fishing. "How convenient," she thought. She counted over twenty boats before she tired of holding up the boy to see and ducked back into their house. But not to rest. She had had enough of that and was anxious to meet her new home.

They had a little game that they played. She would place Ḷainjin on his

---

[42] "They are fishing longline for tuna."

stomach — which he hated — and he would roll himself onto his back and then laugh. They would repeat the game again and again. He never tired of it.

A while later, she watched as their proa approached the reef landward of where most of the fishers were. Many called out to greet the well-known westerners. Others simply raised their arms in acknowledgment. Kāleptak could be seen curling its gentle yet powerful swell into a wave that broke as it spiraled down the reef edge, leaving a turbid line of froth in its wake as it backwashed into the sea. She glanced at Japeba, who cracked the same smile he had earlier.

"He must be planning on surfing us over the reef's edge on the crest of that swell, and he's drawing us closer as the moments pass," she thought. Then, all of a sudden, Jipeba drew the sail tight as a drum, and Japeba steered them nearly perpendicular to the reef edge just as the swell broke on their stern. They seemingly both laughed at her widening eyes as their boat rushed through the froth over the reef's edge and on to the shallow water on the reef itself. The keel bumped on the reef flat, and the two jumped off the boat to steady it through the waves, to a point on the reef where they would have to unload passengers or wait for the incoming tide.

Jipeba suggested that she hand the boy off to him, which she did. It seemed a little too far down for her to jump as they had, so he suggested that she climb down backward and step on his knee. Soon she found herself carrying the boy shoreward through the surf and dipping him in the water, which he loved, and she didn't mind because her skirts were all wet anyway. Other men were coming from shore to help, and soon — with most of the weight now off the proa and the extra help — they were able to lift the boat over the short, natural hump in the reef flat that seemed to trace westward just landward of its edge. The craft could then float shoreward, through a sort of cleared channel on the reef, the rest of the way toward shore.

The reef was unexpectedly broad. Finally, she reached the sand and waited there, surprised there were no women in sight, only handsome men, usually in pairs, tending their canoes, which were lined up on the strand above her. Some men untangled their fishing lines. Others paired up to carry the boats down the beach to the reef.

She laughed to herself. Should she grab one now? The men were mostly surveying her with evasive glances. If she weren't so shy, she would say, "Hello! It's me… Helkena from Wōtto." She felt liberated in her new environment.

She held the boy up to look around. "Handsome men everywhere, but you will be the handsomest, the strongest, the most knowledgeable of them all! Won't you?" She put his face close to hers until he laughed. "Yes, you will! Yes, you will!"

She was watching the brothers slowly walk the proa shoreward on the reef, still partially flooded, when two young women suddenly approached her. They seemed to appear from nowhere.

The women greeted each other. "*Iọkwe*!"[43]

"*Iọkwe*!"

"Are you from Wōtto?" asked the more forward of the two. "How bad was the storm? We heard about it over a moon ago. We knew Japeba had gone looking for his daughter. Do you know what happened to her? Who's this?" one asked, snatching Ḷainjin from Helkena's arms.

The second woman didn't say a word. She just smiled warmly and tilted her head, as if to say, "It's just her way."

"Such a beautiful child! But not yours, obviously. Whose?" The woman now holding the boy didn't wait for an answer. "Tarmālu's. This must be Tarmālu's child. And they've brought you here from Wōtto to help take care of him."

Since she had asked and answered her own questions with only a nod or two from Helkena, what else to say?

"They call us the 'girls of the ocean side.' We were watching all the fishermen from our *jikin bojak*[44] over there." Still holding the boy and pointing with her nose to an area of trees and underbrush just to the south, she added, "Oh girl, you must be bursting. Let's give you a visit." She began walking, taking the boy with her. Helkena had no choice but to follow. After passing under several tall coconut trees, they entered an unruly tangle of brush that smelled of defecation. "Squat anywhere. Men don't come here. Only us women."

Helkena squatted to relieve herself. "Girls of the ocean side?" The water

---

[43] "Aloha"; "hello (or good-bye), love."

[44] A place for excretion.

burst from beneath her raised pandanus skirts.

"They call us that because our chores are completed here, but we live far away from the village by the lagoon. We live on the ocean side of *pāllep*,[45] close to the western brothers. Our families are their workers. *Pāllep* is their *mọrojinkwōt*[46] from the *irooj*."[47]

Helkena had heard the term but forgot what it meant. Not to fear, her new, intrusive friend came to her aid.

Touching Helkena's arm, the quieter of the two explained. "That means it was granted as a spoil of war. Apparently, in his younger days, that Japeba was a fierce fighter. The other, I'm not so sure."

Removing a few leaves that blocked her view of the beach, the ocean-side woman, still holding Ḷainjin, remarked, "There they go now. There's enough water left on the reef for them to walk the proa over by their boathouse. They're inseparable, those two. Father says we're lucky to have them here. Japeba is not as demanding as the previous *aḷap*[48] was."

"What happens to the previous *aḷap*?" Helkena stood and tightened her skirts around her.

"They become *rijerbal*[49] like the rest of us. Only they sit and seethe like a jāpe full of *nen*[50] tea. But they know it's their own fault," the outspoken woman answered.

"They didn't step up and fight when their time came," chimed in her companion for the first time. "Now they're more embarrassed than anything."

"*Pāllep* is a big strip of land. The island is widest there," added the brash one. "There's a swamp in the middle, and the ocean side is broad, like a slice of *jāānkun* cut in quarters."

Though Helkena found her informative, this woman's overbearing

---

[45] Aka "pāllep wāto"; a specific tract of land from ocean to lagoon on Namorik Atoll.

[46] Aḷap rights given for bravery in battle.

[47] Chief.

[48] A paramount landholder who manages land on behalf of an irooj.

[49] Worker; commoner

[50] Either the fruit from *Morinda citrifolia*, a small tree prized throughout the islands for its medicinal properties, or the tree itself; a tonic thought to promote health. Also called "noni" among Polynesians.

attitude was annoying.

Then she announced, "Oh, here he comes!"

"Who?" asked Helkena.

"Just the most... I'm going... How do I look? Hair up or down?"

"Down," said her friend.

"Child or no?"

"Child. He's a conversation piece."

Without hesitation, the young woman stepped out of the brush and into the open and began walking toward the fisherman's boat.

"She's been working on him for moons now," declared her companion.

"What's her name?" Helkena asked.

"Libwiro."

"Is she always so..."

"Take charge? Yes, always! But she's very good at what she does."

"What's that?"

The girl laughed, as though Helkena had asked something amusing. "I'll let her explain."

"Well, it looks like Japeba is moving his craft up the reef. I better follow him to our new home. I hope she doesn't mind me taking Ḷainjin back."

With that, Helkena departed their *jikin bojak* and walked over to the strand, where a young man was preparing his canoe and talking to Libwiro. "Thanks for holding my boy for me. I'll take him back now. As you can see, Japeba is leading us off to our new home." Then she smiled broadly at the young man. "I'm the girl he brought from Wōtto to care for his grandson." He smiled back as she took the boy and traipsed down the beach.

Helkena turned back once, only to see the young man still assessing her, and raised her arm to acknowledge him. Perhaps to Libwiro's chagrin, he reciprocated.

The beach was all sand, very wide and much steeper than the beach at Wōtto. But walking the proa up the reef was slow going, so she soon caught up and trekked along the wet sand a little above the two brothers until she could no longer endure the heat of the day. The long shoreline curled off into the horizon. The tide's wash, clear as it lazily swept the shore, cooled her feet and ankles. She tried shading the boy with his mother's half-skirt wrap, but he cried every time, preferring the sun despite the extreme heat. When she lowered his feet into the water, he splashed and giggled.

After a while, they came to their destination, a large pole house high up on the strand, overlooking the beach. To the right were a large, partially open-sided cookhouse and then a series of boathouses. The first, and largest, was empty. Several men and women poured off the strand, where they had been waiting, and trod down the beach to greet the two famous elders and help them lug their catch shoreward. Their craft was methodically hauled up the beach to its boathouse.

Helkena watched all this as she slowly trudged up the beach. The houses had been kept in good maintenance and the grounds manicured even in the absence of the *aļap*.

Japeba soon began to fillet generous pieces of fish from his brother's catch and place them on strips of freshly cut banana leaves. She recalled Japeba's words: "We have much breadfruit and freshwater taro swamps and many flavors of pandanus."

"Apparently they have an abundance of banana trees here too," she thought, marveling at his action. No one on Wōtto would do such a thing. Bananas were rare there, and their leaves considered precious, at least until they turned yellow. On Wōtto, all the banana trees, heavily composted due to the poor soil, were in the village. She looked about for them. Sure enough, she found a broad stand of them growing inland of the main house, with another just east of the cookhouse. "See, they're protected in the shadow of this thatch from the salt of a west wind. Clever, no?" she told Ļainjin. How large and green they were. She had never seen banana trees so large. She held the boy up to the patch and away from her. That was his signal to urinate, and he did so. She decided that this would be his place to urinate from now on. She would bring one of her customs from her beloved Wōtto, where they composted their banana plants. That was unnecessary here on Naṃdik. Suddenly, she felt a moment of nostalgia for the brown-leafed island she had left. What were her mother and father doing right now? Had her daily tasks been shared equally between her mother and sister?

Turning away from the banana trees, she was surprised to see the two "ocean-side girls" sitting with the other women, perhaps to take their family's share of the recently filleted tuna. They smiled at her coyly though she couldn't guess why. She wondered how they had arrived so fast and then looked back at the wide beach, realizing that they had taken the much shorter path walking down the strand. Were they chiding her because she had walked the longer distance? If they were to be her only friends, fine, but no more "taking charge." She could lead her own life, thank you. And right now, there was too much to see, and too much to learn about two kindly, somewhat mysterious men.

Japeba prioritized the distribution of tuna to his rijerbal while it was still fresh. His cutting board, once a hull plank, still bore the drilled holes showing its lashings. From head to tail, he separated the pink flesh of the *bwebwe*[51] from its backbone with his shell knife before cutting the equally sized chunks that he placed on the banana leaves. He cut all the pieces from all the tuna before distributing them to the women who sat waiting on the coral-pebble floor beneath the big house. The east wall of the cookhouse behind the banana patch sheltered a bin for firewood that mostly held empty coconut shells. His cookhouse was quite long and enclosed three separate firepits, each with its own neat pile of the carefully selected hard-coral stones used to absorb the heat of its fire and bake its contents. A lashed rack with several shelves stood next to the firewood bin and held several jāpe of various sizes.

In the meantime, his brother was leading the methodical process of hauling the proa up the shore to its empty boathouse. Helkena heard him initiating the chant, followed by a chorus response from the men hauling, who lifted the craft as they chanted and nudged it shoreward one step at a time.

She left Japeba to his work and walked over to the open-sided boathouse. The two other boathouses both held resting outrigger canoes — one a medium-sized proa and the other a much smaller canoe, like the ones she had seen fishing. They had rolled the sail of the medium-sized proa onto its

[51] Yellowfin tuna: Neothunnus macropterus.

rojak[52] and neatly stowed it above the craft, on the roof's crossbeams. Skinny mangrove poles were also stored there. The proa's two paddles lay crossed on its outrigger platform. The fishing line and lure were neatly wound around its rectangular spool, the length of a forearm. The *lem* was there inside the hull, and the mast, with all lines attached, lay horizontal over the length of the hull, its *pāp* rollers piled on the sand in the corner. Even the club they used to succumb the wild tuna lay at the bottom of the hull, all high and dry. Everything was ready to launch at a moment's notice.

These men were perfectionists. "They did what was necessary, and they did it well," she thought. For seasons to come, every man and woman from Wōtto would vouch for that.

Then she walked around the large pole house that was their main home. It had a single entrance in the middle of the floor that was itself made of mangrove poles of uniform size. These two men had pulled up the single ladder that serviced the entranceway to prevent rats from entering the home. The shutters along the windward wall promised to cool the inside with what breeze there was when opened. Would she sleep up there with them? They had also spread out well-worn *jepko*[53] beneath the house, and a small group of women, seven or so, was sitting upon them. The mats gave the house a homey, lived-in look.

The heat was surprising. The boy was wet in her arms, and beads of sweat dripped from her forehead. They were on the ocean side, and of course, the island itself ate the cool air that blew off the lagoon, blocking it with its trees and underbrush. Helkena looked over at the women patiently sitting beneath the house, conversing and waiting for their piece of fish, and to a person, they were wafting trimmed breadfruit leaves at their faces. She handed the child back to the ocean-side girls and sauntered over to one of the large breadfruit trees surrounding the large courtyard. She picked up a fallen leaf, trimmed it down, and began fanning herself. After retrieving the boy, she fanned his face too.

"The heat here is so..."

---

[52] The yard or lateral boom of the triangular lateen sail. Vertical boom: rojak ṃaan; lateral boom: rojakkōrā.

[53] Mats plaited with the whole pandanus leaf.

"Wet?" One of the women finished Helkena's sentence as she sat down.

"Yes, that's a good way to describe it."

"I bet the heat up on Wōtto is drier," the woman added.

"Yes, that must be why the sweat is pouring off me like rain."

"Wait till it rains! It gets so cold you'll shiver under your jaki." The woman motioned to a youth nearby. "Boy, cut down a bunch of L̗ōj̗apeba's[54] coconuts for us women."

The youth glanced over at Japeba, who pointed with his nose to a nearby tree. Up the boy scrambled, and soon the green nuts were pounding the courtyard pebbles. He found a husking stake nearby and soon brought Helkena, who let Ḷainjin drink first, a wet, husked nut to cool her down. Later, the boy passed coconuts to all the women.

Then Japeba passed out the fish until there was nothing left. "Perhaps he would receive their share from those rijerbal now fishing," she thought.

The women sat and socialized a bit, and after a while, they each headed home with a nice chunk of tuna. Before leaving, Libwiro and her companion promised to return before dawn to escort Helkena to the ocean reef to *kabojak*.[55]

"How did they know where she would be sleeping?" she wondered.

Later that afternoon, Japeba's rijerbal each brought him a fish, which the *aļap* quickly cut up into strips that he put into a jāpe. While he was doing this, his brother sat on a *raanke*[56] and grated several mature coconuts. He dampened these grindings with water to make coconut milk and then squeezed it over the freshly cut tuna. Then he squeezed a dozen limes over the mixture and added salt. Helkena had seen limes before. Even tasted one. Tarmālu had brought them, but they wouldn't grow on Wōtto. Jipeba let the mixture sit for a while to let the limes "cook" the raw tuna, as he referred to the process. Then he served it with some freshly roasted breadfruits brought by a neighbor. It was the most delicious meal she had ever had.

After supper, Jipeba announced that Helkena and Ḷainjin would have the

---

[54] The male prefix "Ḷō," when placed before a man's name, shows respect, like the female prefix, "Li."

[55] To make ready; to eliminate.

[56] A stool-like apparatus shaped like a saddle with a protruding arm capped with a semi-circular shell grater.

big house to themselves. He and his brother always slept in the cookhouse anyway. Before dark, the women of the ocean side came back singing and conducted an impromptu *kaṃōḷo*[57] for her. They circled her as they sang, and each presented her with a little welcome gift. She received fans and pretty shell necklaces.

Later, she climbed the ladder with the sleeping boy. The inside of the house was like theirs on Wōtto before the storm. When she opened the window flaps on the east side of the house, in came the remaining light of the long day and a faint breeze. After propping these ones open, she went to the opposite side, by the ocean, and did the same. But the prop sticks on this side were longer, allowing her to prop the windows up fully to expose the horizon, which was starting to turn colors. "What a wonderful place for a house," she thought. They had covered the floor with jaki, and the mangrove poles beneath gave way slightly beneath her step.

She propped the boy between her legs so they could both see the expanse before them. The light from the crescent moon in the middle of the horizon seemed to cut a path across the ocean straight onto the broad reef and straight toward them, as though they were the only ones looking. Watching the moon as its sliver of light slowly set into the sea, she felt welcome. "This is your new home, Ḷainjin," she said.

It was a fitting end to an adventurous day. But her body ached from the trip's leveraging of new muscles and bones, and the long night's darkness passed too quickly.

Libwiro, the woman who had promised the day before to wake her, came by and stood below a window on the east side of the house before dawn. "Psst."

"I'm over here. Middle window," Helkena murmured back. She sat up next to the sleeping boy.

Libwiro's head soon popped through the window from outside and into the dim light of the shell lamp in the corner of the house. "Ready?"

"Is it really morning already?"

"Yes, the sun will be up shortly. You better get your butt out there unless you want it to shine or unless you can hold it all day. Libujin will stay with

---

[57] A newcomer celebration.

the boy."

"So that's her name," thought Helkena.

She met Libujin as they crawled in opposite directions across the floor, one going to the ladder in the middle of the loft and one coming from. As soon as Helkena had landed on the mats below, Libwiro grabbed her hand and led her down the beach to the shore.

Helkena had met her type before and felt resistance futile. "This woman is aggressively friendly."

"We always walk down a way from where they launch the boats."

The tide was high and lapping the shore with some turbulence. Both women took a few moments to search the shoreline for smooth, flat stones they could use to wipe their rears. Lifting their dual pandanus half skirts, they squatted in the knee-high water and defecated in the current sweeping the reef.

"Libujin told me that you do something very well."

Libwiro laughed. "Has she been telling stories about me again? Who did she say I sat on? Honestly, that girl gets me in more trouble."

"No, she just said you were good at what you did."

"Oh, well, I guess you could say I have a certain reputation for… You know." She swayed her hips in a circle as she squatted there in the water and then wiped herself clean with saltwater and her stone. When Helkena didn't catch on, she added, "For sitting over them."

"Who?"

"Ehh. Boys, you innocent! And men. Some quite old!" She laughed. "Well, that is a way to develop a reputation around here. The older they are, the more *jukkwe*[58] they've had, and the better to judge."

"Judge?"

"How pleasurable, silly. They just lie back and 'Owoo, owoo, owoo.'" Giggling, she rotated her hips again, lifting her skirts to her waist above the water.

Helkena, remembering her mother's words, asked, "But with more than one man, how do you know who's the father?"

"No father, silly. I don't let them squirt inside me! You can tell when they're

[58] Sand clam; bivalve; word used to refer to one's vagina.

about to spurt — when their eyes roll up into their skull. The polite ones tell you. I finish them off by hand. It's just 'owoo juice.' Not so bad to get a fistful. Wipe it off on their thighs or their breadfruit nuts. They love that!"

Helkena was dumbfounded. She had never in her life heard such talk.

"Now that boy you saw me with yesterday… Him I would gladly let go inside me. And have no others forever after!"

Helkena remembered the way Libwiro had placed her knee on the boy's hull — slightly exposed in an unladylike fashion. It must have been obvious to him what she was after. Part of Helkena was curious as to what this woman would say next. She was a woman, all tattooed and ready. So, there was nothing wrong with such talk, but it was so new to Helkena that she had nothing to say back.

The sunrise was now brightening the horizon above the island, turning the sky a light, clear blue as they trudged slowly back up the beach.

"I can see you're not tattooed, but most girls cheat a little. You've been with boys, right?"

Helkena saw no reason to lie. "No."

"Okay," Libwiro said excitedly. "Then we'll have to fix that, won't we?"

Helkena was silent.

"I learned to *urōk*[59] from Lijitwa, my tattooist."

Helkena remembered the name. "Is that the one who spent many seasons on Āne-pin̄?"

"Oh, yes. She's very good, don't you think?" Libwiro turned her neck and shoulders toward Helkena, showing off her lines in the dim light and stopping for Helkena's inspection.

Helkena had heard the term *urōk* many times. A slang word for "intercourse," its real meaning was to bottom fish from a canoe. She wasn't sure why the word had two meanings. It was probably a joke she didn't understand.

"The brothers promised that they would sponsor my lines and that Lijitwa would be my tattooist."

"Then you're lucky. She doesn't tattoo much anymore. She has only one

---

[59] To fish with a line atop a canoe; slang for "intercourse."

subject this season, a *leerooj*[60] named Argin. Very uppity that one."

"Well, the tide waits for no one. Should we go see her before *rarō*[61] or after?"

"I think we should give the brothers time to raise the subject themselves. After all, they are sponsoring."

"And you don't want to cheat a little bit? I've got just the boy for you!"

"No. I mean, maybe later. I just arrived. No need to rush! Let me adjust to this new place first."

"You sound older than your seasons. Remember, you're only young once!"

Helkena quietly remembered her mother's words: "And you only get one first time!"

They squatted beneath the breadfruit tree a ways from the cookhouse and began collecting the newly fallen leaves.

"Okay, I'll give you your first lesson," Libwiro said. "Squat flat-footed and let your *jukkwe* hang as low as possible. It's hard at first, but it'll get lower over time. Pretend you're sitting over a boy's manhood and teasing just the tip of it, making that thing of yours all wet. Swirl your hips like this, keeping just the tip of his spear kissing your womanhood and making him long for you to plunge down upon him."

Just then, the brothers' fire flared, and Libwiro motioned for her to move to the leaves farther away from the cookhouse to ensure their privacy.

"I don't understand how I prevent him from pushing up into me."

"That's just it. He will try! Oh, will he try, but you're quicker. Besides, what you're doing to him feels so good he's paralyzed by agony. It's all he can manage to just lie there and let you tickle the tip of his spear and hope you'll plunge down upon it. And you will. But only once after a long time and not until he's flailing around like a fish out of water."

"I must admit that sounds fun."

"Girl, that's only the half of it! It's what you can do to that *būtti*[62] of yours that's exciting! That's where Lijitwa comes in. She'll teach you how to

---

[60] Female chief.

[61] Cleanup; collect fallen leaves.

[62] Wart; projection from skin; slang for "clitoris."

leverage your *būtti* like a steering oar to give you the most pleasurable voyage you can imagine."

Just then, the cooking fire turned smoky, and the smoke started drifting their way. "They must have covered their fire with stones," said Libwiro. "They're preparing an oven. We're done here anyway."

They had started back to the house when Jipeba appeared from the inland path carrying netted jekaro shells.

"Jekaro for the boy," he announced, handing Helkena the netted shells.

"Jipeba, is it true you are going to sponsor Lihelkena's[63] lines with Lijitwa?"

"Yes, that's what I promised."

"Well, is it okay if I take her over there today? Just to show her around and such?"

"Yes, that would be fine."

Libwiro flashed an annoying "see what I just accomplished" look, and Helkena had just had her day planned out by this new, audacious mentor.

They returned to the house, which Libujen was enjoying. "Girl, you've got this house all to yourself!" She lay stretched out on the jaki. "My house has so many people it's like an all-day *kaṃōḷo*."

"Without the food!" added Libwiro.

"Fish is the problem," Libujen said. "There's nobody at my house who fishes! Girl, you don't know how lucky you are to live with fishermen."

Ḷainjin was awake now, just lying there on his back, flapping his arms and legs. When Helkena went to pick him up, he cried to let her know. When she took him down to the banana patch, he urinated there and stopped crying.

The two girls were surprised. "What a clever mother you are," remarked Libujen.

"No, he's a clever boy. He taught himself to do that."

"While we're waiting for breakfast, let's go over to Lijitwa's place and begin our discussion," Libwiro proposed.

"I have to feed the boy first. Here, hold him."

Helkena walked over to the cookhouse and, after thanking them for the great night's sleep, asked the two brothers if she could help with anything.

---

[63] The female prefix, "Li," is used to emphasize respect.

When they declined, she asked to borrow Japeba's shell knife. After using it to cut a leaf from one of the many *wūt*[64] plants that lined the inland pathway, she quickly returned the coveted tool to him.

Returning to the house, she used the leaf as a funnel to fill the boy's drinking shell, which she had carefully cleaned the night before. Although he drank with gusto, feeding him took a long time. He drank at his own pace and spent a lot of time baby talking between hole sucking. He sucked a lot of air and needed burping. Libujen seemed fine with the delay. She just lay back and enjoyed her private space. Libwiro, on the other hand, seemed irritated by the whole process. "She must not have little brothers and sisters around her house," thought Helkena.

Later, when she, carrying Ḷainjin, and Libwiro walked down the path by her house, Helkena found she was right. Libwiro was her parents' youngest child. All her brothers and sisters had chosen mates and moved away. She had not learned child care. Ḷainjin was a heavy carry, and she didn't think to offer her relief.

The path to the lagoon was very long because it skirted the swamp in the middle of the island, and Naṃdik, she found, was much wider than Wōtto. As they were about to reach and cross the lagoon pathway, they met none other than Jipeba, who had just come from Lijitwa's place. Apparently, out of respect, he had gone ahead and cleared the details of her engagement before their visit. Helkena felt uneasy that Libwiro had pushed him into this. All she could do was to thank him again.

The lagoon pathway ran off into the distance in both directions. Homes faced the path as far as she could see. Children played, and adults walked from place to place between the pole houses. Elders sat in the spaces beneath them and tended to their chores, twisting twine and plaiting mats. Lijitwa's house was above the lagoon shore of *pālle̦p wāto*,[65] just ahead on the other side of the lagoon pathway. The appearance and construction style were the same as Japeba's on the ocean side, except that her house faced east. It was breezier, her cookhouse was smaller, and there were no boathouses. Helkena marveled again at the small size and shape of the lagoon. It was nearly round,

---

[64] Large-leafed land taro: *Alocasia macrorrhiza.*

[65] Aka "*pāllep.*"

and Naṃdik curled from the west side of the lagoon, where she stood, all the way around to the northeast reef. It would take the whole day to walk there and back. Marmar, in the north, was the atoll's only other islet.

Lijitwa was sitting in the cookhouse when they arrived, heating *nen* tea in a small jāpe on her stone-covered earth oven. She was a trim, good-looking woman with many seasons behind her, and though her breasts sagged with age, her nipples revealed she was childless. Her long, silver-streaked hair was tied neatly in a bun.

As they approached, she held her arms out for the boy at once. Ḷainjin smiled and seemed happy to be handed over. "Japeba's grandson! What a wonderful, pleasant child." She began a game, pretending her hand was a bird that circled and periodically pecked and tickled his belly.

She spoke as they continued to play. "Yes, dear. I would be happy to tap your lines for you. Do you have a face mat?"

"Yes."

"Okay, then all you need is your mother."

"My mother is on Wōtto."

"Of course. So Libwiro here will act as her surrogate."

"Oh, great!" thought Helkena.

Libwiro glanced at Helkena with a conceited "I told you as much" look that left her wondering if she was destined to accept this brash girl as a close friend.

Lijitwa returned the boy to Helkena. "Would you girls like a cup of tea?"

The two looked at each other. "*Koṃṃool*,"[66] said Libwiro.

After twisting three coconut half shells deep into the coral stones surrounding her earth oven, Lijitwa folded her breadfruit-leaf fire stoker around her hand to protect it from the heat of the jāpe and poured the yellowish liquid into each of them.

Helkena had long ago developed a taste for the pungent, nutritious liquid and took a sip.

"So, you're still a virgin," Lijitwa observed.

"Well, yes. I don't have my lines yet. I understand that a lot of girls cheat, but…"

"Please don't be defensive. All the better to wait. We can teach you how

66 "Thank you."

to better enjoy your first experience as we tap your lines. Would that be okay with you?"

"I guess so. I mean yes, definitely!"

"Remember, there's nothing to be embarrassed or modest about here."

With that, Lijitwa lifted her front skirt and exposed her between, plucked of all pubic hairs, and her mons veneris, embellished with an elaborate tattoo. She laughed as the girls stared at her privates and then glanced at each other, surprised at her immodesty. Then they joined her in laughter at the mutual hilarity of the situation.

Helkena turned the boy's head away. "What an unabashedly funny woman," she thought, remembering that image all the way along the long path home.

Lijitwa

The days passed quickly in her new environment, now that Helkena's tattooing had begun. Lijitwa had started tattooing her shoulders with a motif she called *bwilak*.[67] The term came from a fish of that name with brightly colored dorsal fins on its back. Many tattoo designs, she learned, were named after fish. This motif started with a series of nine upward-pointing, equal-sided triangles drawn across her upper chest and then a series of what appeared to be eight upward-pointing arrows (the *bwilak*) across the front and back of her shoulders. At the base of each of these arrow-like motifs were three half-triangles that looked like feathers on either side.

First, Lijitwa drew them with the same black dye she would use to tap color into Helkena's skin. She made the dye from burned coconut husks and a little water, and kept it in a coconut half shell. She used the tail feather of an *ak*[68] to draw the triangles and other designs of the motif. Then she drew a horizontal zigzag line across Helkena's upper chest above the triangle points, with the zig ending just above each triangle's apex and the zag meeting the base of the *bwilak*. This combination of jet-black horizontal triangles and vertical *bwilak* scaling the shoulders from front to back proved striking. It took several days to draw the full motif. Lijitwa drew slowly and meticulously, and her sketches of each *bwilak* were identical and parallel to the next.

At the same time, Lijitwa was drawing lines for the lerooj girl, Argin.

One thing had become clear: the lerooj and Libwiro did not like each other.

---

[67] Surgeonfish: *Naso lituratus*.

[68] The frigate bird: *Fregata magnificens*.

"She's always talking about her boyfriend! Ḷōjurok[69] this and Ḷōjurok that! As though he were the handsomest young man on the island. Well, come to think … he is. *Jeej*! She's supposed to inherit the irooj rights to half the island. She's expected to attract a *likao wūlio*[70] with all that. Just sit on him, make a baby, and shut up about it! That's what I say," exclaimed Libwiro as they walked the path home.

"I don't mind her. She's the first lerooj I've ever talked to," said Helkena.

"Then you should talk to her mother. She's so humble you wouldn't guess who she was. That's the way a lerooj is supposed to be. How did this one grow so conceited? They'll pass this question from one person to the next as the central cord that ties her story together." Libwiro stopped walking. "Give me that boy. I'll carry him a bit for you. He's getting so heavy!"

"It's all that jekaro," Helkena said. "He drinks two full shells with fish in the morning, and it just goes on from there. Bananas, *jokkwōp*[71] — you name it! You know, those two never stop cooking! One then the other! They promised to fatten me up, but I'm not used to eating that much. He's the one getting fat!"

By the time they got back to the cookhouse, the elder brothers had fished, cooked breadfruit, and prepared dinner.

Jipeba complimented her. "Look at those lines! So meticulous. Absolutely perfect! When will you get to use your mother's face mat?"

"Tomorrow, I guess."

"It surprises me she would start tomorrow, with the day of *mama*[72] coming up."

"Day of *mama*?"

"Helkena hasn't heard about the day of *mama*," Jipeba told his brother.

Japeba was scraping roasted breadfruit with a *jukkwe* shell. He had roasted the green skins of the unripe breadfruit to a charred black and was now scraping them down to a delicious, crusty light brown.

Without explanation or further ado, Japeba began his eerie chant.

---

69 Argin's chosen one.

70 Handsome young man.

71 Mashed, cooked breadfruit mixed with coconut milk.

72 To worship the anjilik spirits.

We fly east from Eb.[73] *Sea blows free.*
Bright night returned,
let me debark at Jokdik.[74]
I hang at my place here under —
east seas wander.
They're always sure
to make me their
lure behind —
where my soul
trolls freightless.
If line breaks, I die — waow!

All the while, Japeba scraped the breadfruit with a consistent cadence that accompanied his singing and added an aura of groundedness to this otherworldly chant.

When I die, I have
committed my soul
to wāto[75] *called Kāroka.*[76]
I hang at my place here under —
east seas wander.
They're always sure
to make me their
lure behind —
where my soul
trolls freightless.
If line breaks, I die — waow!

He raised the pitch of his voice at the end of each refrain as though he was the lure they trolled and he the one who risked death.

---

[73] Mythical cannibal isle far to the west.
[74] Islet of Rongelap atoll; means "short perch."
[75] A tract of land from the ocean side to the lagoon side.
[76] Islet of Rongelap Atoll or Rongerik Atoll.

I'm anointed with
his magic perfumed oil.
Smell of jebwatōr![77]
Has powerful spell.

I hang at my place here under —
east seas wander.
They're always sure
to make me their
lure behind —
where my soul
trolls freightless.
If line breaks, I die — waow!

Do you smell tuar,[78]
and kino[79] *and ajet?*[80]
Know Jirabelbel[81]
has cast his death spell.

I hang at my place here under —
east seas wander.
They're always sure
to make me their
lure behind —
where my soul
trolls freightless.
If line breaks, I die — waow!

---

[77] Grated taro mixed with coconut milk, wrapped in taro leaves, and baked in the oven.
[78] A sweet-smelling, plant-based spice.
[79] A fragrant, broadly lobed fern (*Phymatosorus grossus*) often used to spice earth ovens; grows at the base of trees.
[80] Drift nut; sweet smelling; used with coconut oil to make perfume.
[81] An anjilik chief.

Shoot of which leaf should
make my medicine?
Shoot of leaf nen has
power so bitter.

I hang at my place here under —
east seas wander.
They're always sure
to make me their
lure behind —
where my soul
trolls freightless.
If line breaks, I die — waow!

Once Japeba had finished all the stanzas of his song, he passed some breadfruit to his brother, turned to Helkena, and began his tale, which seemed like an explanation.

"There are several skies here in Rālik. One is sky of *ṇoniep.*[82] Another is sky of *anjilik.*[83] When a boat appears in our dreams, we say it was perhaps a boat of anjilik with a crew of anjilik. They come from Eb, the island of Irooj Rilik.[84] They sail eastward and stop first at Odik, an islet of Bikini. Then, after a night or two, they sail to Rongelap and stop at Jokdik. Then, when they leave Jokdik, you know they're headed for Rongerik. They're going there to fish *ṃōlṃōl.*"[85] Japeba was still scraping the roasted breadfruit as he narrated his story.

"You know that night we call *jetkan*, when the moon is among the palm leaves at sunset? Well, that's when they'll come. They beach their *tipñōl*[86] at a *wāto* called Larbit, and those who call them and use their medicine come

[82] People from a spiritual world who live the old life contemporaneously with people of the present day.
[83] Legendary sailors who live in a contemporaneous spirit world and visit on the nights before, during, and after the full moon.
[84] Mythical character; Chief of the West.
[85] A mackerel: Scomber japonicus.
[86] Large outrigger sailing canoe, or proa.

down to the shore. You hear them talking. You don't see them because they're in another sky, but you hear them talking.

"'When did you leave the island of Irooj Rilik?'

"'Oh, about sunset.'

"'How is the irooj?'

"'He wants to eat *m̧ōlm̧ōl*. Has anyone fooled with our coconuts?'

"'No, they're still there.'

"Their coconut tree is on that land called Mwin-kubwe. When the anjilik are away, it's so full of coconuts you can't climb to the crown. When you look next morning, they're all gone. They've taken them along to drink while fishing. While tide is low, they sail up to that islet called Bikinakin and fish those *m̧ōlm̧ōl* there. Then toward morning, as tide rises, they return to Larbit and beach their *tipñōl*. At dawn, you wake up and people of Larbit give you your share. So, you cook your fish and eat a bit. Next night is *jetmar*[87] and next night *jetñōl*,[88] same as night before. They come and fish for three nights and then no more.

"Their leader is called Luwawa. You know that bird we call *kabaj*?[89] The one with a long neck? That one who turns his head sideways like he's spying on you? Well, that is Luwawa. Maybe he is looking you over. If he decides to make you sick, you're gone! Unless, of course, you find someone who knows their medicine.

"The time of the cycle when the moon is full, we celebrate that day. We call it the day of *mama*. Everybody sails to Marmar to worship. People of Wōjjā[90] tell of a man who refused to worship with the others. He went *karōjep*[91] instead. Do you know *karōjep*?" Japeba continued without waiting for her answer.

Helkena just slowly swung her chin from side to side. His words were so few and precise that she would not dare interrupt him now.

"You use a fish bone tied to an empty coconut shell — and a sand-crab arm for bait. You take maybe ten of these and throw them out onto the ocean. Then you wait for flying fish to take the bait.

"One jumps over there, and you paddle," Japeba said. "Then another over

---

[87] The night the moon rises at dusk in the island brush.

[88] The night the moon rises at dusk upon the waves.

[89] Reef heron.

[90] Islet of Aelōñļapļap Atoll.

[91] Fishing for flying fish with coconut-shell floats.

here, and you paddle. On and on, this man who refuses to worship busied himself like that until evening. He had his canoe nearly filled with fish. Then he looked up and saw a huge *tipñōl* paddling toward him. No sail on the huge boat.

"But a man stands up and asks about events on the island. 'What are people doing there?'

"'*Jeej*, nothing much.'

"'Nothing?' he asks.

"The fisherman is silent.

"'They aren't doing anything at all?' he asks again.

"'*Jeej*, well, they're all gathered at north end for day of *mama*.'

"'Then why aren't you with them?'"

Japeba moved his arms dramatically. "Waow! Now the fisherman knows this is an anjilik craft. One measure of his fright: his whole canoe is shaking with him."

Japeba began dramatizing by shaking his body such that it brought a smile to their faces and even Ļainjin began to laugh.

"Now the man says, 'My name is Jebrọ,[92] and the reason why those people worship us is so we don't come and eat you up. All right, look at me. See that man at stern? That is me. You see that man up front. That is me. Now take another look.'

"When the fisherman looks up this time, he sees a hundred faces before him — like a net thrown over his head.

"Jebrọ says, 'That is me! So how can you pretend there is no need to *mama*?'

"Waow! They have ruined him now. Nothing he can do but stare down into the ocean. The man in the boat takes all his fish but gives him one breadfruit seed and orders him to paddle back and plant it.

"'We give you your life,' Jebrọ says, 'but don't ever tell or mention your story of meeting me to anyone, ever. If you do tell, on that day, you die!'

"So, he paddles back to Wōjjā, and he plants his seed as told and never again misses a day of *mama*. That breadfruit tree grows and grows. I've eaten fruit from that tree, and the fruit is different from any other tree in Rālik. Anyway, people keep asking him where he got the seed. But he always

---

[92] Aka Pleiades; constellation. Tenth-born and youngest son of Lōktañūr.

answers that he found it on the ocean side.

"On and on, and then one day, he can't stand it any longer. He walks to ocean side and back to lagoon. He walks from one end of the island to the other. He is all bothered to tell the story. Then, that evening, people gather at his house, and he can't resist telling them. 'Do you remember one day of *mama* long ago...' He tells his story of what happened that day.

"Waow! He falls asleep and never wakes up. Those anjilik squeeze him. Squeeze him. He doubles up like an unborn baby, and they bury him that way — not lying down but sitting up.

"The name of that breadfruit is *kubwe-doul*. Someday you'll visit Wōjjā and eat some and see for yourself how it is different from any other breadfruit in Rālik."

Ending his story just as abruptly as he had started, Japeba transitioned back into his silent mode and said no more.

The breadfruit was delicious and went well with the raw tuna, lime, and coconut milk. The boy even ate a little of the inner breadfruit softened with coconut milk.

For Helkena, the painful part began the next day. She lay prone on the mats outside, in the light beneath Lijitwa's house. The lagoon breeze there kept her cool. Her mother's mat over her face and a stick in her mouth prevented her from screaming.

Lijitwa's ancestors had made her chisel many seasons before, from an albatross bone collected from Eneen-kio.[93] Its ten points had been lashed to the end of the *ñi*,[94] which she mercilessly tapped with her mallet. She had brought these implements with her when she retired from Āne-pin̄. It was Helkena's new friend Libwiro's job to watch Ļainjin, whose favorite stunt was to sit up and crawl off.

The motif over Helkena's shoulders took the next four days to chisel. Then she'd get a rest until her lines healed. They were swollen and, not surprisingly, got infected. Tapping a new line next to an infected one was extremely painful. Lijitwa warned her, as she had from the first day,

---

[93] Wake Island; traditionally the northernmost island of the Ratak chain of the Marshall Islands.

[94] Tattooing chisel made of albatross bone; the sharp teeth of this tool.

to have Japeba administer *wūno*.[95] But she was still a little afraid of him and spent most of her time resting in the empty house and remembering her mother's words, "a woman knows pain!" Lijitwa was also tapping the lerooj named Argin at the same time. Lijitwa would tap one of them, then allow her to rest while she worked on the other. So, a sense of camaraderie built up between the two out of their shared misery. Liargin was swollen too, though not infected. Apparently, she had a whole team of *driwūno*[96] at home to watch over her. Helkena wondered if Liargin would suggest she stop by and have them look. But that invitation was not forthcoming.

When Helkena returned home that evening, with Libwiro carrying Ļainjin, Libwiro mentioned she would be going with her parents to Marmar the next day. When they arrived, Japeba's proa was absent. The next night would be *jetñōl*, and apparently, Japeba had left for Marmar with his brother, assuming correctly that she wouldn't want to be seen by anyone until her lines healed. There was a whole jāpe of fish and breadfruit soup on warm stones that would last her more than two days. Like everything the two made, it was delicious.

After dinner, Libwiro excused herself, and Helkena was alone with the boy. As she looked out at the long shore before her, she noticed a very large swell breaking on the reef's edge. She remembered Japeba saying there were times when kāleptak swelled on the reef, making it impossible to launch or land a proa. Of course, the men had sailed to Marmar by way of the lagoon, so they were unaffected by it. The swells were something to watch, though, each methodically curling deep blue and then crashing and breaking into ragged white froth along the reef's edge.

She decided to take a bath. She went to the well, filled the jāpe several times, and carried her water to the enclosed *kapwōr* shell bathhouse. She washed Ļainjin first. He loved the water and could crawl on the shore all day. While he splashed in the *kapwōr* shell, she grated more coconut to rub her skin. Then, without rubbing her shoulders, she poured coconut milk over them, thinking it would soothe the pain of her infections.

---

[95] Medicine.

[96] Ones who know medicine.

It didn't really, and that night was the most painful yet. Worse still, she felt a fever developing and closed the eastern windows to cancel what breeze was entering the house. She shivered in her mat the long night through.

The following day, she was no better, weaker even, and slept late. Then, after his breakfast, Ḷainjin started crying for the shore. The tide was outgoing, but plenty of backwater had built up against the beach for him to play in. The kāleptak swell was still curling and crashing on the reef's edge. She sat on the beach, feverish but enjoying the warm morning sun and watching him play.

Out in the ocean, she noticed a lone sail bobbing among the swells. She didn't think much about it at first. On a normal day, there could be dozens of sails, but she began thinking. With a swell like that crashing on the reef, how did they get out there in the first place? Then she realized they must have left before the kāleptak current "fell," as they say. They must have gone fishing yesterday morning and gotten stuck out there all day and all night. She noticed something else. The boat was bobbing right around the area where Japeba himself had turned his boat toward the reef and surfed over it. Of course, this swell was much larger than that one must have been, and only one person appeared to be on board. She watched him for some time. "He must be testing his chances and putting off the opportunity again and again," she thought.

What could she do to help? Absolutely nothing. No one, not even Japeba, could help him. She felt bad, knowing that he was all alone out there and probably very, very tired.

Then she realized something else. The tide was retreating. If he didn't cross the hump at the crest of that reef now, he would have to stand on his craft, waiting, till after midday. Picking up the boy, she walked down to where Japeba had come ashore. In a sort of channel there, a craft could be floated over the reef to the beach, so she began carrying the boy onto the reef next to that channel. Although Helkena didn't know whether the man could safely head shoreward after overcoming such a swell, she wanted to show him she was there to help him nudge his craft over the hump on the reef if he got that far. Would such encouragement induce a wrong move against a very dangerous swell? How could anyone expect her to know that? She was just a novice woman, and he could see that for himself.

The man rode the crest of several more swells but then turned and let them roll under him. Not the right one, apparently. Then, as fate would have it, after several more abortive attempts, he decided to go for it. Had her presence encouraged him? She would probably never know. But the wave he had chosen must have been a particularly fat one because he seemed to ride it for a long time, and it was a long time before it broke on his stern, well reefward of the ones preceding it and well shoreward of the one following. When the swell finally broke, the reef — still flooded by the white water of the earlier swell — cushioned his bump. He put his body between the reef and his boat by dexterously jumping into the water to break its momentum, one hand gripping the outrigger platform and the other, the forward hatch. His weight off the boat now, he successfully held it unscathed amid the froth.

That was the first real look she got of him, and she was surprised. His long hair fell on either side of a handsome face. His chest and abdomen looked chiseled, as if made of hardwood. He was tall — and, to top it all off, he was gazing straight at her with understandably distracted yet grateful brown eyes. He suffered cracks in his lips. He looked exhausted. She realized he was thirsty.

"*Iọkwe*!" He addressed her politely, even while fighting the current to keep his boat from lunging forward or being swept into the backwash. He was careful to keep his sail pointed nearly perpendicular to the wind.

"I came to help you. What can I do?" She walked toward him.

"First, let me take that young sailor off your hands and place him here."

Gently taking Ḷainjin from her, the man placed him on the outrigger platform that would lie between them. The boy was ecstatic. "If he falls, there's plenty of water below. When we get to that ridge, see if you can place your shoulders beneath the platform and nudge us over into that channel. Will you be all right doing that? Your shoulders look a little sore."

Forgetting her fever and disregarding the soreness of her infected lines, she did as he suggested. After several tries, as white water swirled around her ankles, they succeeded in overcoming the hump and began walking the boat down the channel toward shore.

"We've got to get wūno on those lines," the man said.

"I'll be okay," she said, looking into his concerned face with determination.

"A woman knows pain, my mother always says."

"That's more than pain. Those will leave scars if we don't treat them."

She hadn't thought of that, but the anticipation of this man intimately applying wūno to her shoulders filled her head with imaginings and crowded out all else.

Smiling, she nodded her consent. He could treat her with wūno — and most certainly, she was willing to subject herself to anything else he had in mind. She tried to take Ḷainjin from the outrigger platform. He would have none of it and, giggling, crawled to the other side, where he sat before the boat's commander.

They spoke only a little after that. Islanders have a way of developing friendships out of silence, and Helkena didn't want any reality intruding on her fantasies. She would come to realize that he knew exactly who she was. News in such a small place travels quickly.

When they got to the water before the shore, he anchored where it was waist high, knowing his boat would float peacefully in the outgoing tide. Ḷainjin complained a little when she pulled him off the boat, but she kept dipping his legs in the water as they walked down the beach.

Then she carried him up the shore to Japeba's cookhouse. She didn't even know the man's name yet but didn't dare ask, not wanting to appear forward.

"Let's get you something to drink," she said, reaching into a basket of husked coconuts the brothers had left her and handing him one.

He quickly poked a hole in its mouth, guzzled its contents, and burped. Then he began searching for something inside the cookhouse and found what he had been looking for. "I knew it had to be here somewhere. Older folks always have this stuff lying around."

He had found a glob of overripe *nen* wrapped in a leaf. He kneeled behind her and tenderly began to apply the overripe mush to the lines on the back of her shoulders with his finger. She nearly collapsed at the feel of his gentle touch caressing the back of her shoulders.

"I don't know how old this is. I guess it doesn't really matter. I've seen my grandmother keep it for a whole season. It never seems to decompose."

He spoke close to her ear in a soft, intimate voice that buckled her back and made her want to lean back against him. Her mind raced to the next phase, when they would be facing each other. What if he kissed her? She opened her mouth at the thought, as though preparing herself. She would lie back on the mat and let him take her then and there. "In front of the boy?" she wondered. "What kind of mother would do that? A desperate one." She stifled a laugh.

"What?" he asked, catching her chuckle. "Trust me, these infections are nothing to laugh at. Are you aware of the smell?"

"Yes." She had smelled the rotten odor from the time she had gone to bed and covered herself with her mat last night. She thought naughtily, "All the better to attract your sympathy. I have something else here that might interest you."

He asked her to turn around, and she was right there, practically in his face with an excited smirk and an embarrassing blush. She was able to study his face as he concentrated on covering every line with the colorless, nearly odorless, mush. She decided he was the most handsome man she had ever seen. He was serious about his work, and she liked that. He would make a good father and an attentive partner. He had deeply cracked lips. "Is that why he isn't kissing me?" she wondered.

She spoke to him silently. "Okay, look at my face now. I'll kiss you with my tongue. I'll moisten your lips with my spittle!" But he kept methodically applying the wūno, from the right side of her collarbone to the left, until every line was covered with goo. Ignoring her pointy, blushing breasts, he rewrapped the glob of *nen* in the same leaf and put it back where he had found it. Then, lying down next to Ḷainjin, he began lifting him up above him, much to the child's amusement.

"Was that it! No kiss?" Helkena wondered.

"I'm very tired." He glanced at her face for the second time. "I was out there a full day and night, and half the next morning. I even circled around to the other side of the island. It was worse over there. When the kāleptak current falls, it falls! But you brought me luck. What possessed you to walk out there?"

"I thought I could help."

"Well, you did. Thank you," he said, putting the boy down. "Now I need to sleep. Is it all right if I sleep here?"

"Of course, but wait! You need to eat first!" She grabbed the jāpe with the fish soup and put it before him.

"I'm hungry, but I can't eat all that."

She hadn't washed the coconut-shell bowl that she had eaten from.

"I'll go wash this," she said and flew back down the beach, chastising herself, to the ocean shore. She began washing the bowl and crude spoon in the sand and warm, clear water left by the retreating tide. For perhaps the first time, she regretted her virginity. Here was the perfect man, and he had fallen into her clutches at the perfect time. It would never get better than this, and she had no idea what to do except feed him.

After washing the eating tools meticulously but with no ideas coming to her, she returned to the house and found him asleep. Ḷainjin looked like he was about to cry, so she took him to the shore and let him play there. All she had to do to make the boy happy was place him at the water's edge, and he took it from there. Of course, not able to walk on his own, he crawled — sometimes even with water over his back, like a little shark. He was amazing. Everyone who saw him said so.

Later, back at the cookhouse up on the strand, she wondered how to advance. In one sense, she was relieved. The man had fallen asleep, so there was nothing to do. At least she could stop chastening herself and just let herself be. Now she didn't have to decide. Well, she could lie down next to him. No, that would be too forward even for a sex-starved novice such as herself. He was very tired, and she had to respect that. Even if she did awaken him, what then? She needed the type of training that Lijitwa had promised, if only to give her the confidence she lacked.

He still hadn't eaten. That would be a good reason for her to sleep in the cookhouse and not in the loft — so she could feed him when he awakened. She hung on to that as her plan. When he woke up, she'd ask him if he was ready to eat. She wanted to return to him now. She could watch him sleep for as many hours as it took. But there was no way she could pry this naked sand crab from his play at the shore.

After a while, though, when he slowed down and crawled up to her, she was able to snatch him and carry him back up the shore to the cookhouse. Her hero was still sleeping, still in the same position on his back. She fed Ḷainjin soup from the freshly washed bowl and watched as he, too, fell asleep. Then, quite tired herself, she walked back down to the beach yet another time, to wash the bowl once again. Her fever was pressing down on her now that the excitement of the day had waned, and she felt weak and ready for a nap herself. Once she had returned to the cookhouse and placed the basket of husked coconuts next to the man, she curled up with the boy a respectable distance away and fell quickly to sleep herself.

The two of them slept through noon and woke mid-afternoon to the sound of the man sucking the water from another of the coconuts. She could hear the tide, and it was time to look after his boat. He stood and looked out at it as he drank.

"I'll help you put it on the shore," she said. "Do you want to eat first?"

"Yes, please. Sorry I fell asleep on you."

Helkena poured soup into the shell cup and handed it to him, along with a wide slice of aerial pandanus root, which he used to brush the breadfruit and fish from the bowl into his mouth. "You must have been tired. I was at the shore for just a short time!"

"I made the mistake of lying back. It only took a moment, I guess."

"Ḷō oceanside there spent the whole morning crawling up and down the beach. He's trying to turn our skin black as night." She turned up the bottom of her mat skirt to show him the light skin above her ankle. "That's what he's done to me!"

"He'll grow up strong and healthy. Soon he'll play with his friends, and you can look out from the shade of the cookhouse and prepare even more food for him. This soup is delicious. Did you make it?"

"The men cook all the food around here. They say my job is just to watch the boy, so that's what I do." She took a fiber of dried coconut husk and tickled Ḷainjin's nose with it. He rubbed it away. When she did it a second time, he awoke, and instead of crying — which was usually his first reaction — he giggled and tried to grab it away.

"Want to go down by the ocean?"

When the boy sat up and outstretched his arms, she picked him up, and off they went, the three of them walking down the beach. "Now's the time to take my hand," she thought. She was walking close to him and even bumped her hand against his, but he didn't catch on.

"It looks like kāleptak is still swelling on the western reef. How long can it linger there?" she asked.

"It's unusual for a girl to know about kāleptak. But I guess you pick up that sort of thing by being around those peculiar brothers."

"What's peculiar about them?"

"Did you hear about the way they raised their daughter, Tarmālu?"

"Yes, they blindfolded her and took her down to Diaj and led her around the rock until she knew everything. What's peculiar about that?"

"Nothing, I guess. I have great respect for them. It's just... You've got to admit that is unusual."

"Well, they're talking about teaching the boy the same way now."

He took Ḷainjin away from her. "This rascal here!" The boy giggled as the strong man set him on his hip and carried him along. "Japeba's chosen one died, so I guess he had reasons why he never took another. But the one they call Jipeba. Isn't it peculiar that he never chose anyone?"

"No more peculiar than me coming here from Wōtto to give you the particulars. You're from this island. You should know. He has chosen somebody, only they keep it secret for some reason. I think she likes it that way. Have you ever heard of a tattooist called Jitwa?"

"No! Really?"

"It's true! Not so peculiar as you thought!"

When they got to where he had anchored his craft, they let the boy play on the shore, and together, they beached the canoe. But this time, the man lifted the front of the boat on his shoulders and had her lift the stern hull so the wūno he had applied to her shoulders was undisturbed. It took them a good while to nudge his boat passed the high-tide mark. She struggled with the weight of the stern, but when he asked how she was doing, she nodded and smiled. Finally, his boat was in its place, and she had retrieved the boy from the shore.

The man had untied his *rojak* and began to roll his sail around them. He was preparing to leave her. Suddenly, her insides were torn, and her thoughts were in a panic.

"Thank you for everything." His smile was genuine. With his sail wrapped around his long *rojak,* over his shoulder, he walked down the path.

Ḷainjin looked sad. This was another lesson for them both. Goodbyes were sometimes easy, sometimes hard. She felt stunned, and angry at herself, but she didn't know why. What more could she have done to entangle him? She must ask Libwiro, who had an opinion on everything. Suddenly, the full weight of Helkena's fever overwhelmed her. She returned by way of the path along the strand, where she washed the eating utensils one more time. Then they entered the house, and the boy, perhaps sensing her sickness, allowed her to sleep undisturbed in the dark. Her beloved, brown-leafed island seemed farther away now. She could see that life here would draw her in. Well, at least she had met a man who was worth capturing. All she had to do was figure out how.

Jipeba's advice

Helkena awoke from her deep slumber with the boy's hands on her face. She felt sore all over, but it was morning already. She carried Ḷainjin below to the banana patch, and he burst out a steady stream of clear liquid. He had obviously waited for her to waken. "You are one sensitive, unselfish child," she said.

The tide was high on the reef. Walking oceanward down the shore, she glanced around curiously, checking for her new friend's boat. Instead, a sail fluttering in the distance caught her attention. Farther down the reef, she saw a craft sailing with its *kubaak* nearly upon the shore. It must be Japeba's proa returning from Marmar. And there, of course, above the high-tide mark where they had hauled it, sat the proa of her chosen one.

Her shoulders weren't quite as painful as they had been, and her fever seemed to have lessened. The night's rest had been good for her, and the wūno must be working. She pleasantly recalled the man's gentle, methodic touch. Now she had a good reason for not wanting her lines to scar. She wanted to look perfect for him.

She tore off a wilted tuft of *kōņņat*[97] leaves from a branch. She had broken them but a few days before and carried the heavy boy a good way down the beach from where the brothers would be landing. The boy took his cue from this as soon as she placed him on the shore. He crawled to the edge of the breaking waves, defecated, and crawled back along the shore, leaving his remnants to dissolve as the surf pounded the sand behind him. She wiped

[97] A short, sprawling tree that grows next to the shore; beach cabbage: *Scaevola taccada*; "naupaka" in Hawaiian.

his rear clean with water and the wilted leaves and glanced again at Japeba's craft. It had hardly moved.

She thought he must be spilling air as he cautiously continued along the shore and realized there would be time to fire up his ground ovens.

She placed the boy on the matting in the middle of the cookhouse floor with his toys: several polished coconut shells and mangrove sticks and an old *anidep*.[98] Normally, they would trade time kicking and crawling down the *anidep*, but she had work to do now. Quickly rounding the courtyard, covered with beach stones, she picked up the fallen breadfruit leaves and stacked them next to the three ground ovens in the cookhouse. The elders had left the ovens dug and the firewood and tinder stored in their bin at the eastern head of the cookhouse. She built her fire frames and took a dried, partially shredded *utak*[99] to the only flame — a shell lamp of coconut oil — in the compound, in its place in the corner of the loft.

The brothers had made the lamp from two coconut half shells. They had cut off the rounded end of the one facing down so the other one, the cup, could rest inside. The two were glued together with breadfruit sap. The cup was filled to the brim with oil, its wick of coir sennet coiled at its center.

She moved the lamp to a west window and back from the outside, and lit the partially shredded end of *utak*, once folded. Once it was lit, she wafted the flame through the air on her way back over to the cookhouse and lit her three fires. As the tinder burned, she kept adding dried coconut shells until they burned into piles of hot coals. Once the last of the successive shells had flared, she covered them with the previously used oven stones, which were stored in mounds next to the firepits, completing her project just as Japeba's proa finally arrived.

Helkena grabbed Ḷainjin, rushed down the sand to help them, and put him in the water to play. The crew had brought a large *kilōk*[100] of *or*[101] they

---

[98] A foot-sized cube of woven pandanus leaves that is kicked back and forth within a circle by clapping participants.

[99] The bud sheath from which the composite coconut flower will burst. (It shoots up between a coconut frond and the tree trunk and splits open to reveal the flower buds that become coconuts. The sheath's stem eventually rots and falls off to the ground.)

[100] A strong, trapezoid-shaped basket plaited from the central portion of a coconut leaf. It features braided handles.

[101] Spiny lobster: Panuliris penicillatus.

had apparently gathered from the reef off Marmar the night before, and several other *kilōk* of husked *iu*.[102] These lay on the outrigger platform and needed unloading before the proa could beach. Grasping the one filled with *or*, she lugged it up the shore to the cookhouse. She passed Jipeba carrying another on her way down the beach and took the final *kilōk* off the platform. That one contained *iu* and was much heavier than the first. She had to rest halfway up the beach, and Jipeba relieved her of it upon his return. She turned back to help nudge the proa shoreward, keeping her eye on the boy, who was contentedly playing tag with the surf. Proud that her idea to light the ovens would prove useful, she helped push the boat a few more steps up the beach. As the tide had reached its peak, there was no reason to continue further. Japeba would wait for his workers to help later. They even left the sail hanging to dry in the morning sun.

Japeba was quick to notice the redness on her shoulders and seemed impressed with the way her friend had applied the wūno. "Who did this?" he asked.

"A friend," she answered vaguely.

Perhaps he assumed she meant Libwiro because he replied, "She did a good job, but I have to wash it down with hot tea and then reapply the ripened *nen*."

At once, she recalled her new friend's welcome touch. If it was up to her, she'd leave his wūno untouched forever! She recalled the old people saying, "The lines will be the thing a man or woman sees with their last breath." But she resolved she would remember his gentle touch instead.

Jipeba brought the boy from the shore and began to play kick-and-crawl *anidep* with him. Japeba attended his jekaro trees and then set about steaming a combination of *or* and *iu* in the largest oven, where he would bake them in their own juices. Very carefully, he covered everything with several layers of the breadfruit leaves she had gathered earlier and, finally, covered the whole pile with clean beach sand. On another of her ovens, he placed a small jāpe filled with sweet groundwater, into which he had sliced four or five unripe *nen*. These he had gathered in the orchard of *nen* he had planted beneath his jekaro trees. On the third oven, he placed a second small

102 Often referred to as "coconut apple"; a sprouted coconut.

jāpe to heat Ḷainjin's jekaro. Having hung unharvested since the night before, it had already begun to ferment.

Later, when the tea got hot, Japeba poured a coconut-shell cup for each of them. Then he began cleaning away the wūno applied to her shoulders the day before with the hot *nen* water and a piece of *inpel*[103] he had retrieved from one of his jekaro trees. As he applied his own wūno, she vowed to wipe all remembrance of this application from her mind and, henceforth, remember only the touch of the original application by her chosen one.

Soon the *or* were well steamed, and one by one, Japeba carefully removed the broad, sand-covered leaves to expose the bright red insects of the sea.

Later that afternoon, Libwiro arrived during the boy's nap, and Helkena blurted out the entire story with all the details of what had happened while she was alone at the compound. "What should I have done differently?"

Libwiro's answer was immediate. "When you turned up your skirt to show him the light skin above your ankle, you should have shown him more of your leg for one thing. That would have got his juice percolating. You were too modest. Don't forget, he still considered you an untattooed woman. He accepted you for the young girl you are. But then you let your girlish modesty stand in the way of a glorious sexual experience. Next time, show him you are a woman ready for him to ravish!"

"That's it! You are right! I was too modest. I lost my chance."

"That's all right. You'll get him next time."

"What if he never comes back?"

"He will come back. He's a man of honor. Even if he doesn't see you as someone he could seduce, he won't just pretend you never met. He'll be back at least one more time. That's when you can make your move. But now I'm curious. I wish you would have gone ahead and asked his name."

"I was trying not to appear too forward!"

"Well, that was your problem."

"Yes, I realize that now. I can show his boat to you. Will you recognize it?"

"Probably, let's go."

"I have to wait for Ḷainjin to wake up."

---

[103] The fibrous, cloth-like outer sheathing of the coconut flower buds found at the crowns of coconut trees; used to squeeze milk-like oil from coconut gratings.

"Ḷainjin, Ḷainjin, Ḷainjin! He's another splash of cold water on your sex life."

Helkena turned cross at this suggestion. Truly, this woman was crass, and sometimes she was thoughtless. But she was an only child, and that explained most of it. Deciding not to dignify that statement with a response, she just lay back and pretended to go to sleep next to her charge. The boy slept for a short while longer and then woke with a big smile, as though his dream had been a pleasant one.

"*Kwo kenan ke etal nan lik*?"[104] she asked him. She had been teaching him how to speak.

"*Lik*,"[105] he replied.

In the meantime, Libwiro had gone to the cookhouse and was in the mess of eating a lobster when they appeared from the house, on their way shoreward. Several *iu* were broken open before her, and lobster gook spread her fingers wide.

"We'll wait for you on the beach," Helkena told her politely. She had already decided they would walk along the shoreline to make the boy happy, much to the consternation of her friend, whom she knew would rather take the shortcut along the strand. But then she had to come down to the beach anyway, to scrub her hands in the sand.

It was noon and the tide had completely drained from the reef, leaving only backwater that filled the crevices and low spots. With no surf sloshing onto the shore, this was one of the tides of the moon Ḷainjin seemed to like the least. That would all change, she thought, when he got old enough to carry a pole and fish at the reef's edge. By that time — or shortly thereafter — he'd be on his own, and she'd be back on Wōtto raising her own family with whatever-his-name-is. So, she kept him in her arms despite his attempts to wriggle free. She was determined to carry him to the boat landing, where the water on the reef was deeper and he could play. There were a hundred sharp things on a dry reef to scratch his tender skin. "You can wait a quarter of a day for the reef to fill again," she told him.

Libwiro caught up just then, overtaking her by surprise. "Point his boat

---

[104] "Do you want to go oceanside?"
[105] Oceanside.

out, and I'll go take a look."

Helkena pointed at the boat, off to itself, up the beach but just over the high-tide mark. "It's over there."

"You're kidding! That looks like Ḷōjurok's boat." Libwiro ran up the beach to make sure.

Helkena had heard the name before but couldn't… "Oh no! That's the name of Liargin's chosen one. He must be the one she's always talking about."

"Yes," Libwiro called back. "That's Ḷōjurok's boat. Are you sure?"

Of course she was sure. How could she forget? Feeling sick and dizzy, she sat down on the sand, turning away from her friend and the boat — everything. She needed to think. Was that why he was so polite? One wrong move, and he was certain Liargin would hear about it. How could she compete with that pretty little lerooj? She couldn't. Her dream had been but a footprint in the sand, destined to wash away with the incoming tide. What a letdown!

Uncharacteristically, Libwiro turned sensitive, realizing Helkena needed to be alone. "I'll see you back at the house. It's hot out here!"

Helkena, lost in thought, couldn't even acknowledge her friend's departure. She blamed the whole mishap on her virginity. Why hadn't she taken Libwiro's advice from the beginning and found some man — any man — and just gotten it over with? Then, when the right one came along… Smack! She would be ready to wrap her arms around him, and not let go, and not give him up. "That little chiefess has everything! Why does she need my chosen one?" she thought.

She could half hear Liargin speaking and imagined she would say, "But I chose him first." Helkena had no argument for that. Hadn't she just arrived on this island? She was supposed to accept things the way they were.

Ḷainjin took her attention away. He had found another shell for her to hold and crawled down the reef, looking for others. He was learning to sort of walk now. At times, his own buoyancy held him upright.

The next few days passed differently from the days before. It was as though she had awakened from her careless adolescence to the reality of womanhood. Once Lijitwa had completed the tattooing of her arms, she drew and tattooed a single squiggle on each finger, right down to the base of her nails. Finally came the part Helkena now wanted the most, the tattoo on her mons pubis. For this, they moved to the bathhouse, which had an open roof for plenty of sunlight. Helkena had to pluck every single pubic hair and used — but what else? — a *jukkwe*! She hid her activity, even so far as collecting the hairs, in her own bathhouse while Jipeba played with the boy. By now, Helkena was so accustomed to the bite of the chisel that she had permanently discarded her mother's face mat. Lijitwa told others Helkena had a smile on her face during the whole mons pubis process. That tattoo, of course, would only be viewed by her sexual mates or perhaps by whichever intimate female friends she wished to show it to. It was not a tattoo for the average woman, and it would symbolize the completion of her associated sexual training.

Helkena was determined to learn the "art of fulfillment," as Lijitwa intriguingly referred to it. Certainly, this brusque woman had the perfect personality to teach her about men. Helkena's first and permanent assignment was to pick up every leaf that fell every morning — no rest. So, she started getting up before dawn and picking up every breadfruit leaf and every other leaf that happened to fall on their broad, pebbled courtyard. Some mornings, she even went over to Libwiro's and did her work as well. The idea was to strengthen her legs and get into the habit of squatting not on her toes but flat-footed. She was to raise herself after each leaf and squat all the way down for the next, with her private part lowered as close to the ground as possible until that position became second nature. Squatting that low was the hard part, especially when bound up in a two-piece skirt. It took a lot of practice to get all the way to the ground, but she was determined, and Lijitwa made her prove her abilities.

The rest of the instruction was pretty much conversational. Lijitwa emphasized she had to develop the "want," or she wouldn't secrete enough juice from her *jukkwe* to lubricate the procedure properly. The "want" would come from daydreaming and touching herself down there. She must not be embarrassed by the "want." She must cultivate it like a rare breadfruit or pandanus cutting that she had to water daily.

Lijitwa warned her to avoid concentrating on personalities in her daydreams, but rather to focus on her mission, the object she was to tease. She would say, "Concentrate solely on the mast you must gradually impale yourself upon, and at the same time, agitate your *būtti* and bring yourself closer to fulfillment, like an itch that's finally scratched. Only once realized will you finally allow your partner that wet discharge he is so desperate to achieve. Forget about who your partner is. Your partner is irrelevant to your pleasure! We'll give you one moon to prepare yourself, and then we'll schedule your first encounter."

"First encounter with who?"

"That's my point. It doesn't matter! You're only learning the motions. Like learning to sail a boat. It doesn't matter whose boat. It could be Jipeba's."

Helkena laughed at the suggestion.

Lijitwa's eyes twinkled. "Don't be so quick to laugh. He comes up here to dig for *jukkwe* all the time."

"Yeah, I thought you two had something going on. It seems to me like he'd be quite a gentle partner."

"He gets no pity from me! He calls me Mānnijepḷā[106] and pleads, 'Come land on me just one time!' And I respond, 'Hold on, sailor. I'm at the helm now!'"

So, every night for the entire moon, she lifted her skirts and followed instructions. Though she had seen a boy's private parts and could only imagine a man's erection, want would never be a problem. Based on Lijitwa's descriptions, her imagination did the trick for her. Sexuality gradually overcame the fear of losing her virginity. She always imagined it was Ḷōjurok seducing her. Of course, she was nervous about a rendezvous with anyone else. What if she hated him? What if he smelled bad or was ugly? This would be the real thing. However nervous, she was looking forward to this first encounter. She looked at it as something necessary to get over.

Moons had passed when she decided that her imaginary love affair was over. The season of *añōnrak*[107] was over. The season of *añōneañ*[108] had fallen and blew strong and relentlessly from the east. Living on the westernmost part of the island, she wasn't much affected — except by the

---

[106] A mythic bird that flew passengers from one island to another.
[107] "Call of the south"; the northern solstice, which annually coincides with summer in the northern hemisphere.
[108] "Call of the north"; the southern solstice, which annually coincides with winter in the northern hemisphere.

lack of rain. She noticed the wind mostly when she visited Lijitwa. It swept the lagoon, brought surf up the shore, and covered everything with a thin layer of salt spray.

She had met Ḷōjurok once again when he came by Lijitwa's to walk Liargin home. Somehow, Helkena assumed Liargin had asked him to come so she could show him off. Nothing was said about their brief time together. There was nothing to say, really, except the part where he took her throat and discarded it in the banana patch before he walked away.

"No, I did that myself," she thought. In truth, he was blameless. In another moon or two, rumors spread that Liargin was pregnant, and that was just more salt in her wounds. But it served to heal her all the faster, like a fish that had stolen her lure. What good would it do to feel remorse? In truth, she'd never had him. So, why feel rejected?

Her first little tryst was with a lad who seemed younger than she. Set up by Lijitwa, it was on a moonless night. He came to her window in the pitch darkness before dawn. She left Ḷainjin sleeping where he lay and went below the window where he was sleeping to engage the man. He was but a boy, and once she'd figured out how young and inexperienced he was, she soon felt at ease and her jitters subsided.

They sat on the mats below the house. Afraid of talking and waking the elders in the cookhouse, she let her actions speak for themselves. Following instructions, she touched him very softly, and his manhood sprang up against his somewhat-soft belly. Everything progressed as planned. She levered it straight up as she hovered over him, pocketed it into place, and began the swirling motion Lijitwa had taught her. She liked the erotic feeling of their naked private parts rubbing exactly where she wanted. But she was just starting to imagine he was Ḷōjurok and preparing to plunge down and break her hymen when he moaned, wet himself, and went limp. After he made her promise not to tell Lijitwa of his cock-like performance, he left and that was it. She felt like a hen shaking herself up off the ground, not satisfied but perhaps feeling better than nothing, and better still that she had been on top and had momentarily taken charge of the disappointing affair.

Later that day, she decided to seek Jipeba's advice. She thought he had noticed she'd turned a little despondent, and her latest adventure hadn't cheered her up any. "Do you remember that day you came back from Marmar to find my shoulders infected, and someone had applied wūno?"

"Yes, I remember that. It wasn't Libwiro though, was it?"

"No, it was Ḷōjurok. I helped him land his proa when the kāleptak swell fell over the western coast. I thought we shared a moment, but I didn't hear from him again, and then Liargin got pregnant, and I'm just starting to get my bearings again."

"Men are different from women. A woman always chooses the sensible, practical path. Not so the man. He turns wherever his throat points. There, chew on that for a while. It's my word of wisdom for you to consider as you age. Anyway, Ḷainjin will be walking soon, so it's time he started his instruction."

"What instruction?"

"The *jeḷā*.[109] It means 'knowledge.' Knowledge of your position at sea, compared to the islands that may or may not surround you."

"How was a boy that young supposed to learn such things?" she wondered. It seemed ridiculous to her, but Jipeba was serious as always, so she listened.

"We will start out by sailing at high tide to Diaj," he explained.

She knew that was the big rock they had seen on the reef between Naṃdik and Marmar.

"This would be his first center of learning. We could take Ḷainjin alone, or you could come along, keep him company, and learn the *jeḷā* yourself."

She thought of the miserable seasickness she had experienced on her trip from Wōtto. Did he mean that, this time, she would be outside the little house that they had dismantled? She supposed so. Then she remembered how cold Japeba's place at the helm had seemed. This was a big decision.

"You mean learn to sail, to take the helm myself?"

"Yes, in time."

So not at first. Well, if it was too much for her, she could always say so later. "I'll come along," she said bravely, and that was that.

The *jeḷā* training started shortly thereafter. The brothers placed Ḷainjin in a large jāpe normally used to mash large quantities of *bwiro*. It had holes

---

[109] A navigator's knowledge of their position at sea related to the islands that may or may not surround them.

as handles on each side. They tied a rope through one of these handles and towed the jāpe behind their proa, sailing down the shore at high tide until they reached the end of the island. There, they met the strong wind and tide that swept the reef. Spilling air from their sail, they slowly approached the rock. Then they dropped their sail and, with much difficulty, paddled their proa around and around the rock with the boy in tow. The water was rough and the air brisk and chilly.

Yes, she pimpled up when the tide splashed her bare breasts and the añōneañ winds blew upon her. The boy appeared cold and frightened, and he cried at being by himself in the jāpe. But the experience was short, and that was all there was to it. His grandfathers treated it as something of great importance and did it nearly every day during the quarters of the moon when the tides were highest. They were pleased with his progress.

Ḷainjin did get accustomed to the experience but learned very little as far as Helkena could see. She, on the other hand, picked up some valuable boat handling experience.

The brothers even began letting her steer the boat to Marmar on the days of *mama*. The wind was often quite strong, and this put lots of pressure on the steering paddle. It took all her strength to keep the boat on course. And yes, it was cold but again, only lasted a short time. Luckily, it was always high tide, so they didn't have to weave around the coral heads that, over the centuries, had grown up to the surface of the lagoon.

Jipeba always tended the sheet and instructed her the whole time. He commented on her skin dimpling up as she shivered. "You must eat more fish to keep your body heated." She grew proud of her performance and took his advice.

Each family that participated in the *mama* had built a crude shelter on Marmar. Not every family, she found out, took part in or even believed in anjilik medicine. Travel to the islet seemed mostly an outing to fish, collect crabs, and rest.

Japeba chanted one of his anjilik prayers. Lijitwa did not attend. Neither did Liargin or her chosen one.

Marmar was a beautiful island with many birds and an abundance of corals and sea life. It had a saltwater swamp in its interior, so many of the participants cut mangrove poles and carried them back to Naṃdik.

In time, Lijitwa arranged her second encounter, at her house in the middle of the afternoon. This time, it was with a man nearly twice her age. "When is she going to get to the eligible bachelors?" Helkena wondered. This man obviously had a chosen one and probably several children. Nevertheless, she lowered her skirts with a smile, and as soon as he saw her naked before him, with her tattoo in his face, his private part sprang up even before she touched it. She squatted over him, drew his manhood up straight beneath her, and pocketed it — again, exactly where she wanted. She swirled her hips round and round, then for the fun of it, plunged herself down onto him. She felt her hymen break and was glad to be rid of it. This man had staying power, and unlike the boy Lijitwa had sent her, he had bathed and knew not to wet himself at once. But in the dim light of Lijitwa's loft, she was having a hard time imagining he was Ḷōjurok. After much rotating, the tip of his manhood sliding around her *būtti*, she had almost reached fulfillment as she gazed into his agonized face, accepting him finally for who he was. But then he started to moan. So, she reluctantly slipped to one side, grabbed his erupting manhood, and squeezed it repeatedly, as Lijitwa had taught her. Of course, she didn't want to get pregnant. She laughed intimately with him as he spurted again and again. He tried to kiss her, but she'd had enough. She wrapped her skirts around herself, thanked him, and went down the ladder.

Lijitwa criticized her. "So short a time."

"Well, at least this one broke my hymen. I liked it, but not him really. Why pick a man so old?"

"Because he's the type of normally discreet man who people believe. If he mentions your tryst to another — and trust me, he won't be able to keep it to himself for long — who knows on whose ears his report will ultimately fall."

"Ḷōjurok?"

"He's Ḷōjurok's uncle. On his mother's side! Such relations are known to talk of such things, are they not?"

Helkena grabbed the boy and began the long slog home.

She recalled later that this was the last time she'd had to carry him. He was walking short distances now, and in the moons that followed, his baby legs straightened rapidly. Soon he was running up and down the beach and swimming like a shark in the ocean tides and playing in the rain.

And oh, did it rain — for whole days at a time. So much rain it reminded her of the typhoon she'd lived through. Except there was no wind with this rain. It poured straight down, and it calmed even the ocean swells. It poured night and day. She had never seen such rain, and never would on Wōtto.

Yet she remembered her brown-leafed island with fondness. She missed her parents and wondered if her sister had taken Tokki yet.

For Ļainjin's first birthday, his grandfathers had planned an island-wide *keemem.*[110] As the moons of añōneañ faded and the rains and variable winds of añōnrak arrived, she marveled at the huge surplus of breadfruit the island produced. The fruit ripened and fell from the trees. Daily, the brothers gathered the surplus of breadfruits yet to fully ripen and mashed them in the same gigantic jāpe they floated the boy in. Then they buried each batch in holes lined with rocks and covered them with breadfruit leaves and sand. This *bwiro*, along with a turtle captured along the sparsely populated eastern side of the island, became the primary food for the *keemem*.

When pregnant Liargin got word of the island-wide *keemem*, she sent her chosen one, Ļōjurok, to *kōṃkōṃ ma*[111] for the event. He showed up early one day with a *kōṃkōṃ* pole — the length of three men — and sat down for a hot cup of *nen* tea with Japeba before beginning his chore. Japeba's breadfruit groves were immense and extended along the path from ocean to lagoon. Each tree held hundreds of the green fruits, some round and others oval. They were nearly ripe but, for *bwiro*, had to be picked at just the right stage of ripeness. Ļōjurok's job would be to climb each tree, fell its nearly ripe fruit, pack it into *kilōk*, and then lug these baskets to Japeba's ocean-side compound for processing.

Helkena was busy with the boy along the shore and wouldn't have even known Ļōjurok had appeared were it not for Libwiro. She had seen him walk

---

[110] The first birthday feast after the passing of two seasons or thirteen cycles of the moon.

[111] To harvest breadfruit by twisting its stalk with a small stake tied diagonally to the end of a long pole.

by her house and ran to alert her.

"What are you doing down here? Your hero is up at the house, sitting with Japeba. I think he's here for the day!"

"Why should I care?" Helkena asked. Then she realized how much she did. "What should I do?"

"Go up there and say 'Hi! What brings you to the ocean side?'"

That's exactly what she did, and when Libwiro found out, she asked if it would it be all right for them to follow along and weave the *kilōk* for him.

So, Helkena found herself walking down the path next to him again with nothing much to say, like before. Only this time, she had more confidence and poise.

"How's Liargin doing?" she asked, and then could have drowned herself for starting with the wrong question. She chastised herself. Why bring her up? Why remind him?

"Oh, she's doing fine. She has several more moons to go yet."

"You moved your boat!" she exclaimed.

"Yes, I sailed it around to the lagoon. We've been trading a lot of our time over on the *rārōk*[112] side. Liargin has land over there."

Helkena couldn't help herself from asking, now that she had already reminded him of the lerooj. "So how's chosen life treating you?"

"To be truthful, it's a lot of work."

"Not a bad response," she thought. At least he hadn't said anything definitely positive.

Then he asked something totally unexpected. "So, how's your search going?"

"You mean my search for somebody to take me back to Wōtto? Why would a man from a wet island give that up to live on a dry one?"

"Yes, you've got a point there, but for love, you can expect a man to do anything."

"Well, at least I've apparently got the word out. When the time comes, I'm sure I can count on Japeba for that. But yes, I'm still looking, and no, I'm not having any success."

---

[112] Uninhabited land.

He didn't offer any suggestions, and they had arrived at the first tree. After giving her the small adze he had tied to his belt, up he went. She got a good look at his muscular legs as he climbed. She was proud of herself for answering truthfully and wondered what had made him ask that.

She looked around for a mid-sized sapling coconut tree and cut off a lower limb to plait its leaflets into a *kilōk*. She notched its midriff in two places and began plaiting the trapezoid-shaped basket.

Libwiro arrived with Ḷainjin. "How'd it go?"

"Well enough! He complains that chosen life is lot of work."

"So, that's positive. Did he suggest you two take a little pleasure break in the bush?"

"*Jeej*! Don't I wish."

Soon the breadfruit, which grew close to the ends of the branches, began falling as he twisted their stems with his *kōṃkōṃ* pole. Once he had harvested that tree, he was able to climb two more while they collected the fallen fruits and filled two more *kilōk*. At one point, he came down and rested among them. Ḷainjin toddled up to him at once.

"You're getting big, sailor!" The boy beamed.

In her usual brash way, Libwiro asked, "How do you occupy yourself these days now that your girlfriend is" — she paused, pretending to search for the word — "unavailable."

"I go fishing a lot."

"Oh really. Well, if you ever come up here to fish along the ocean side, I know somebody who might be interested in going with you." She glanced at Helkena, who threw a small stone from the path at her.

"I'll keep that in mind," he said, smiling.

"Also keep in mind that us women of Naṃdik are soft," said Libwiro. "Women from Wōtto are hard, with lots of muscles in the right places."

He laughed, then joined in the tease. "I know, they helped me once with my boat. Rumor has it they've been trained how to hover in the air like a bird."

This made Helkena blush even more. All the more so having learned that the word had gotten out so soon.

Ḷainjin followed Ḷōjurok to the next tree and held up his arms. So,

Ḷōjurok put him on his hip, leaned his *kōṃkōṃ* against the tree, and climbed to the first outbranch. There, he placed the child at the junction of branch and tree. That made him happy and proud, and he looked down at the women with obvious pleasure.

Before long, Ḷōjurok had felled more than his quota for daily processing. Helkena had a chance to show off her considerable strength carrying the *kilōk* of breadfruit back to the cookhouse, where the brothers skinned the fruit with cut and sharpened cowrie shells. After a while, Ḷōjurok excused himself and headed back down the path. Libwiro encouraged Helkena to walk with him, but she hesitated again and lost her chance. After she saw him at the *keemem*, that would be it — as it turned out — for many seasons.

During his second year of training, the brothers made a pandanus-leaf blindfold for Ḷainjin, and they covered his eyes as they paddled around the rock. They did this until, no matter which way they turned, he was always able to point to it. Their instructions became more verbal as he began to talk. Though they didn't blindfold her, somehow, she managed to pick up the *jeḷā* herself. She learned how to locate the rock based on their explanations of the wave patterns around it and became expert at sailing their craft along the ocean-side shore at high tide.

In Ḷainjin's his third year, the brothers led Helkena and Ḷainjin into the ocean and had her sail them around the island. By the end of year three, she was a better sailor than most men on the island. Sailing fostered the air she breathed and the nourishment she consumed. As she sailed, the brothers took turns hauling in fish, which they would "cook" in the sun and eat raw, along with the breadfruit they brought along for lunch or dinner. What they didn't eat raw, they baked in their ground ovens and ate the next day. Just like Jipeba had told her, she found that the fish kept her body warm even in the winds of añōneañ or the coldest of storms.

On days when they weren't at sea, she began cooking the dishes that the brothers liked, and she learned to prepare them exactly the way they wanted them. She smiled remembering Jipeba's words "don't think we plan to make a servant of you." She was glad to serve them. It made her feel useful. She had grown to love and respect the two men almost more than her own parents. There was no more talk of all the men who would make "pests of themselves." Perhaps they had heard of her occasional "encounters" and assumed that her search for a chosen one was continuing apace. Nothing could be further from the truth. Known only to Lijitwa, and perhaps Libwiro, was that she was having no luck.

She remembered telling Jipeba, "Oh, I'm not picky."

But the truth was that she had become very picky and was becoming more so as her quest for fulfillment became less and less likely to succeed. One after another of the eligible bachelors left her sometimes impressed but ultimately unsatisfied. None could reach the imaginary "Ļōjurok standard" that she set for them.

Not that she didn't enjoy these encounters, but they didn't succeed the way she could pleasure herself. Her other problem was very real despite Jipeba's words to the contrary: "The men of Naṃdik are like men everywhere. Just looking for a good piece of land to supply security for their daughters and a place to raise their sons."

Life on Wōtto was harsh compared to Naṃdik — which was in the middle of a rain belt, apparently — and most men here knew it. It sometimes rained here for days. There, rain was a luxury that rarely lasted a day and only during the moons of añōnrak. Naṃdik men might be willing to lie back and let her swirl and pleasure them from above, but would they be willing to follow her back to her home island and share her life there? She wouldn't know until she asked, and she wouldn't even suggest such a thing until one at least brought her to "fulfillment."

In the meantime, Ļainjin had become a talkative, questioning young lad. He loved to listen to his grandfathers' stories more than anything and even began falling asleep with them in the cookhouse. Long ago, when he'd started calling her Mother, she had corrected him. She would say, "I'm not your mother. I'm just taking care of you for her. She's somewhere out there in the ocean. You have to grow up fast and learn the *jeļā* to find her." What else was she supposed to say to him? She told him about Wōtto and the trip to Naṃdik. He didn't remember any of that. In the summer of his fifth year, after they had circumnavigated Naṃdik many times and had studied the swells originating from the quadrants, all four of them set off for the bird island Kili. This was a small island to the east.

As always, Helkena was at the helm, Jipeba was tending the sheet, and Japeba and the boy were huddled in the doorway of the little house they had constructed on the outrigger platform for her privacy. They had left Naṃdik in the middle of the night and were expecting landfall well before dark the next evening. Stars filled the sky, with the wind moderate from the southeast. Liṃanṃan,[113] when visible, was over their *kubaak* to north. They sailed tight to the wind northeast until dawn, and then, after a breakfast of roasted breadfruit, fish, and coconuts, Japeba began his instruction.

"Kili is due east of Naṃdik," he told Ḷainjin. "I showed you from the stars — and you can see from the sunrise — that the wind has been steady a little south of east, but not south enough to make landfall on a single tack. So, we must tack south, but when and how far?"

"Kili is a bird island, so we tack when we see birds?" The boy answered with a question.

"Good guess. The birds will tell us we're close, and in the evening, they'll point us to the direction of the island, but we'll need to *diak*[114] before then. Look at this swell crossing our path from the east. That is buñtokrear, and it's passing north of our destination island and is unobstructed by it. Remember how it looks now. Because once we tack south and pass through the shadow of the island and feel kāleptak at our stern to lee, we'll come out of the shadow on the south side and face the same buñtokrear with no kāleptak again."

"How do we know we're north of the bird island?" asked Ḷainjin.

"It's a process of elimination. First, we know we're not west of the island yet because we can't feel kāleptak yet. It can only be detected when we're in its shadow."

Ḷainjin persisted. "How do we know we're not south of the island?"

Japeba continued with his train of thought. "Second, we know we're north of the island because we haven't passed though the shadow, which

---

[113] A name: "woman beautiful." "Li": the female prefix; "ṃanṃan": "very beautiful." The north star, Polaris.

[114] To tack or, more specifically, shunt. The tack of the sail is transported from one end of the canoe to the other, keeping the outrigger to windward.

we're about to do once we tack south."

To emphasize that, Jipeba released the sheet, and the boy ran to release the *bal*[115] at the bow. He waited there for Japeba to grab the point of the triangular sail and carry it to the stern end, where Helkena guided it down and allowed the boy to secure it. She handed the steering oar to Japeba, and he set the same tight course a little east of south.

After a while, Japeba asked them, "Do you notice anything different?"

Ḷainjin, the first to respond, demonstrated what he had been taught by pointing south of east. "The island is over there because the shape of buñtokrear is changing. It's not as steep."

Helkena didn't notice anything at first. But as the time passed, she, too, could see the swell from the east lessen more and more as their proa passed though the shadow created on the water by the island.

"Now concentrate on the lift from our lee," Japeba said. "An intermittent swell is passing under us. That's kāleptak, and its period is much longer than that of buñtokrear. You can only feel it here, west of the island, when the island itself cuts off its counterswell."

Ḷainjin nodded and then started counting the kāleptak swells to show he felt them as they passed beneath their craft. He kept counting slowly as the time passed. Helkena could feel nothing, but then she hadn't been in the jāpe, blindfolded, all those seasons.

"Okay, Helkena, you take the helm now. Ḷainjin will tell you when it's time to *diak*."

Ḷainjin loved that responsibility. For his young age, he was very reliable. To Helkena, it seemed the boy had adopted each grandfather as a father figure in his young life. Sometimes, without being as taciturn, he imitated Japeba's silent mannerisms.

They watched the sea around them gradually calm as buñtokrear, the swell from the east, became less sharp and forceful. When Japeba pointed out its counterswell, kāleptak, it gradually became clear to Ḷainjin. Although Helkena couldn't detect kāleptak, she did feel the boat rise at times when Japeba identified it and the boy counted it.

---

[115] The foot between the clew of the lateen sail where its vertical gaff and horizontal yard join.

Many birds began to appear from different directions, so the boy started counting those and naming them as they flew by: *jekad*,[116] *pejwak*,[117] *mejo̱*.[118] But the big birds, *nana*[119] and *ak*, were his favorites, and the ones he never tired of pointing out.

This state of the sea held for much of the morning as Helkena steered them as close to the wind as possible on their southernly course. Then the sea started getting rough as buñtokrear appeared again, building from the east. Ḷainjin called the *diak*, and she took the helm at the other end of their craft. They headed off on a northeast tack again.

Japeba praised them. "Not bad! I would have continued a little farther, but this should get us there."

This time, they stayed in the island's buñtokrear shadow a lot longer. Although they could see flocks of birds swarming from all directions, the majority were flying eastward.

By late afternoon, Kili appeared to the east. It wasn't an atoll but a small single island out in the middle of nowhere. They tacked twice more with the island in sight and, by early evening, had crossed the reef on the north side of the island. Helkena held her breath as she steered them over the blue corals and through the sparkling white water at the reef's edge.

"We could have circled the island and maybe found the swells a little less sharp somewhere else," Japeba said. "But from experience, they fall with a little more forgiveness here."

The din from the birds was distracting, and circling birds darkened the sky above the island. Their poop was everywhere, so they camped on the sand close to their craft. Even then, a white spot would occasionally drop from the sky and land on one or the other, and the group would break out in laughter. Land, after such a long trip, felt good.

One of the first things Japeba did was start a fire. He removed his fire bow and *bwijinbwije*[120] from the proa, searched the strand for a suitable fire

---

[116] Black noddy: *Anous minutus.*

[117] Brown noddy: *Anous stolidus.*

[118] White tern: *Gygis alba.*

[119] Red-footed booby: *Sula sula.*

[120] A by-product of the rope-making process; densely packed strands of coconut-husk fibers too thin for rope making; used for kindling as well as washing.

stick, and went to work drilling his hardwood spindle into the dried, broken-off *kōṇṇat* branch he found there. He began to chant:

Sear stick, blow coal,
fire flame, so fear me!
Eat fire, eat stick,
eat Lairi. Fart!

Helkena was surprised that Japeba was so familiar with the story of Lairi and Likoropjen, a story from her island. The twinkle was back in his eyes as he smiled boyishly and sang the chant from the story of the spirit Likoropjen and her humorous struggle with Lairi, the legendary fisher boy from Wōtto.

It took Japeba no time to create a tiny coal that he dropped into his little wad of *bwijinbwije*. He then placed the smoldering wad between two dry pieces of coconut husk he had brought from Naṃdik. He puffed into them and then wafted them through the air until they erupted into flame. Later, as the coals of his fire matured, he placed stones on top of them and then brought four breadfruits from the boat and began roasting them.

Later, as Japeba was scraping the blackened skin from them with a shell, Helkena began to wonder what else they were going to eat. They could have batted birds right out of the air. A whole flock of them was flying chest high over nests at the island's end. They could have gathered eggs to bake, but Jipeba had another idea. After lighting the end of a *pāle*[121] in the fire, he took Ļainjin toward the island's interior. They returned a while later with four *barulep*,[122] one in each of their hands.

"They're everywhere!" cried the boy. He went on and on about how they had picked the biggest ones, except some were too big for his hands to grab hold of and pick up.

Japeba roasted the *barulep* on the coals, and soon the rich smell of the coconut oil leaking from their bellies onto the hot stones began filling the air. Helkena plaited baskets for their meals and broke open the large

[121] Dried, braided coconut leaves used as torches for fishing; a coconut frond.
[122] Coconut crab.

pincers with hard stones that Jipeba had found along the shore. The best part was dipping the roasted breadfruit into the hand-sized abdomen filled with digested coconut. The crabs, a rarity on populated islands, were quite a delicacy.

Fortunately, the weather stayed clear that night. The next day, they explored the island's shores, dug freshly laid turtle eggs, and ate the tough but tasty little breasts of broiled seabirds. They let the turtles alone because they didn't have the irooj's permission to bother them.

Their return trip began in the middle of the night. This time, they would be approaching their island from the east, and though their destination was much larger, the skills necessary to detect it beneath the horizon differed. Japeba pointed out how the shape of the buñtokrear swell changed as the island blocked its faint counterswell, kāleptak. "Buñtokrear will become sharper and more dominant, as will buñtokiōñ on the northwest tack and buñtokrōk on the southwest tack."

But no matter how many times Japeba pointed these swell indicators out to her, Helkena couldn't feel or see exactly what he was talking about. Ḷainjin, on the other hand, seemed to follow what he was saying. She had her hands full just keeping the sail pointed downwind. The wind had picked up a little and puffed their sail to such an extent that it became difficult to control the vessel.

"*Tiliej*,"[123] crooned Japeba. He had her release the sheet, and the boat naturally turned in the waves to face the wind with its *kubaak* to starboard. Then he stood before the mast and drew in the *tiliej* line a little to reduce the sail's surface facing the wind into two deep pockets.

Ḷainjin had many questions about this. "What's the purpose of that?"

"It spills the wind's pressure from the sail, by reducing the surface directly facing the wind," Japeba responded.

"Why reduce the pressure? Won't we just sail slower?"

"It relieves the water pressure on the oar, making it easier for Helkena to steer," Japeba said.

Ḷainjin persisted. "How does it relieve the pressure on the oar?"

---

[123] A reefing line running up the mast and tied midway along the sail's boom, or "rojakkōrā," to draw it closer to the vertical boom, or "rojak ṃaan."

"By reducing the pressure on the sail."

And it was so. Helkena did find it much easier to steer. She found steering more complicated on this tack. The wind wanted to blow the sail back in its direction, so she had to put a lot of pressure on her oar to prevent that, but too much pressure would put the sail in danger of backwinding. She noticed that yes, the *tiliej* device did make this operation easier. Buñtokrear, coming from behind, was pushing her vessel down into the trough between its swells. So, at a certain point, she had to steer the craft on an angle so as not to plunge her bow directly into the back of the preceding swell, but rather to climb it on a slant. The *tiliej* gave this process maneuverability. It was easier to control the proa.

By early afternoon, Japeba had pointed out another swell approaching on their lee. "That's buñtokiōñ," he said. "It's still somewhat faint because the island is just starting to cut off its counterswell coming from the south."

"Buñtokrōk!" said Ḷainjin proudly.

"That's right!" Japeba acknowledged. "Remember when we towed you east of the rock Diaj, and buñtokrear formed a ridge to the east that seemed to bend around its east side? Buñtokiōñ is doing the same thing now from the north, and its outer edge as it approaches the island is what you can faintly detect lifting our craft to lee. Can you count the swells?" he asked.

Ḷainjin started counting. It was obvious that even though he missed a few, according to Japeba, he was well on his way to becoming a *rijeḷā*, even at such a young age.

Japeba directed Helkena to put buñtokrear on the left corner of her stern and buñtokiōñ on the right corner and to let these two swells "push them home." Although she didn't recognize buñtokiōñ, she turned the craft to what she thought was the southwest, and after another half an afternoon's sail, the atoll appeared directly off their bow.

By late afternoon, with the help of their rijerbal, they were hauling their proa up the beach into its boathouse, and Japeba was distributing bird and turtle eggs to his rijerbal. Helkena climbed the ladder, went early to her mat, and fell quickly to sleep. She was proud of herself and felt stronger and more experienced at sea.

Japeba was a good teacher, but a relentless one. A few weeks later, they took a trip to Epoon,[124] south-southeast of Naṃdik. This time, due to the further distance, they left at sunset on a course just east of south. The wind was firm from the southeast, so it was another moderately close-hauled sail. Japeba assigned Helkena to the helm again, and she climbed the swells lengthwise, one after the other, keeping them on her left and sailing up their front and down their back as they rolled westward.

These weren't the sharp swells of añōneañ they had braved on their way from Wōtto, but the blunt swells of añōnrak. They were to target the northwest corner of the horizon surrounding the island, where — according to Japeba — they could put buñtokiōñ on their left stern and kāleptak on their right. Japeba faced backward the whole trip and, by manipulating the sheet, kept Liṃanṃan — when she peeked low on the horizon between the clouds off their stern — to the right.

Midway through the night, Jipeba relieved Helkena at the helm, and she slept soundly with the boy in their little hut on the outrigger platform. Then, before dawn, Japeba summoned them to one of his persistent lessons of the sea.

Speaking primarily to Ḷainjin, he asked, "Do you feel the swell from the north? It lifts our stern ever so gently. That's buñtokiōñ. We're north of the island, and the island itself is starting to cut off its counterswell from the south. As we get closer, you'll notice kāleptak gently slapping our hull to lee. You will say, 'But we're still north of the island, and its counterswell has yet to be cut off.' And I will say, 'Such is the mystery of the sea.'"

"Japeba," the boy asked for the umpteenth time, "where do these swells come from again?"

"They come from the quadrants. You know that. And they're the result of wind. As you travel south, sooner or later, the wind begins to blow from that direction. Same when you sail north. Unlike buñtokrear, the wind that generated them no longer predominates in this part of the world."

Ḷainjin, always questioning, asked him, "What about kāleptak?"

"Kāleptak is a different kind of swell. It doesn't come from wind but from current. There's a stream in the middle of the ocean that runs counter to buñtokrear. Sometimes it runs a little north, sometimes a little south. Sometimes it gets stronger, sometimes weaker. There are places in the ocean

---

[124] Aka Ebon. A neighboring atoll seventy-three miles south-southwest of Namorik.

where the wind dies out, and in those places, there is a strong eastward-running current. That's where all swells lose their peaks and the kāleptak current runs east with great strength."

Ḷainjin grinned. "It's like the swells of buñtokrear pile up somewhere, and that's their way of returning that water back to the east."

Helkena saw Jipeba and Japeba share a glance, and then they both acknowledged his comment with nods, as though to say, "You precocious boy. You may be right."

She was never able to detect either buñtokiōñ or kāleptak though Ḷainjin could, and he was the first to point out the island, which was straight ahead and exactly where Japeba had said it would be. As they approached the atoll, Jipeba's line got his first strike. He pulled in three more tuna, delaying their arrival but ensuring they would not *depet āne*.[125]

Epoon's lagoon appeared smaller than Wōtto's yet larger than Naṃdik's, but its land mass was much larger, with more islets. Its single passageway to the ocean, on the western side of the atoll, wound between two oddly shaped islets and sported four different coral-structured lagoon entrances, all facing east. Entering the lagoon by one of these routes would mean heading north through a swift current and then trading half the morning tacking through one or another of these narrow entrances — yet ending up near the middle of the lagoon north of Epoon islet.

Instead, since their stay was to be short, they sailed right up to the island's northwestern coast. They crossed the reef there, landed on its sandy oceanfront, and beached amid the plethora of fishing canoes already there. Japeba asked four of the young men gathered there to help carry the tuna. He and his brother carried the enormous basket of *bwiro*, and all four of them set off, rounding the tip of the island and then walking up the strand path to the *ṃōn kweiḷọk*[126] found in the middle of the compound of the *iroojḷapḷap*.[127] The lushness of this place, coupled with the beauty of the calm, circular lagoon, indelibly tattooed the island on Helkena's mind as the

---

125 "Pierce islet," from the proverb "Wa jab depet āne." Literally, "Boat does not pierce islet." This proverb means that a canoe's hull does not pierce the sand of an islet without bearing gifts.

126 Meeting house.

127 Paramount chief.

most desirable place to live she had ever seen. Yet the magnificence of her current surroundings only served to sharpen her longing for home.

The irooj, who was out and about, welcomed Japeba and his brother heartily and led the group to the *m̧ōn kweiļo̧k*, where many of his *aļap* and loyal rijerbal had gathered. Japeba, obviously one of the irooj's favored rijerbal, had not visited Epoon for a few seasons, so they began catching up at once. Japeba introduced Ļainjin, and the irooj made a big explanation of how he knew his mother, and they went on from there. Ļainjin never seemed to tire of asking questions about her, and the *iroojļapļap* was politely ready to answer each. However, he had offered them the use of his compound, so Helkena left them talking and set out to take her bath.

She was about to ask for coconuts and a *raanke* but decided to explore the bathhouse first. It had been erected next to a lush banana patch and was in plain sight. Sure enough, inside the open-roofed structure, among a neat stack of husked coconuts, were a basket of plumeria flowers and a pile of fallen breadfruit leaves that had been gathered. She walked to the nearby well and plunged the jāpe into the water at its bottom. The jāpe had a stone tied at one lip and a *kapwōr* ring tied to its rope handle to keep the water-filled container level as it was hoisted. She poured the water into one of several giant-clam shells placed in a semicircle at the end of the bathhouse and returned to the well several times until all the shells had been filled. Then she closed the door, squatted, and released a pent-up stream onto the thick bed of beach stones that comprised the floor.

Now feeling much relieved, she sat on the *raanke* and tapped the midsection of a large coconut on the edge of a rock placed for that purpose. She split the coconut exactly in half and began grating its meat onto one of the breadfruit leaves. "This is going to be a two-coconut bath," she thought.

Salt had caked over her body from head to foot. She scrubbed herself clean with the grated coconut and flower petals, which mixed with water. Her body and hair were covered with an oily sheen that soothed her sunburned skin, and she smelled fresh enough to eat. The well water was even sweeter than it was on Nam̧dik and a world's difference from the brackish water she had gotten used to on Wōtto. Finally, she wrapped herself again in the same two-piece skirts, which covered her legs to her ankles. She was grateful for the lovely bath and decided to fill the giant-clam shells for the next bather.

When she returned to the *m̧ōn kweiļo̧k*, the irooj and Japeba were in animated conversation. The irooj at once recognized her presence with a smile. "Japeba has been chanting your praises as an apprentice. I can see that you'll make a strong partner for some lucky islander!"

Helkena hadn't thought of herself as an apprentice. "That's all I need, more wild promises. Where are these lucky islanders?" she wondered. "Can't they see I'm more than ready?"

"Japeba tells a lot of stories," she said. "I'm still trying to figure out if they're true. I'm just a *pejpetok*[128] from Wōtto. All my lands are there, where it hardly rains, the well water is hard, and the bananas — if they survive — are very small."

"I've been to Wōtto," the irooj said. "Many seasons ago, probably before you were born. They have groves of lovely pandanus there. It's a great place to find *jāānkun*."

"Well yes, pandanus we do have."

"And you have the legend of Lairi and Likoropjen, and a huge bay on a reef that nearly cuts the island in two."

"That's the part Likoropjen ate! My grandfather told me that story nearly every night before bed."

The irooj laughed. "Here we tell the story of the ņoniep. Have you heard about them?"

"No," she said to be polite, though she had heard of the ņoniep before. Ļainjin, though he'd had a long day, perked up at the notion of a new tale.

"Japeba tells the story of anjilik and their spirit sky," the irooj began. "Most of us are afraid of them because we don't want them to ruin us. But there is one more sky here in Rālik. We call it ņoniep. They don't ruin us but bring good luck. I've never heard any story where the ņoniep ruin anyone. They aren't angry spirits. They know how to love us and live just like our ancestors did, only they don't fight and kill each other. They live in peace from age to age. All the stories I've heard tell how they help us and teach us.

"You know that fishing we do with a pole on the edge of the ocean reef

---

[128] The spent core of a pandanus kernel drifting about in the ocean; a drifter.

at night, when the tide is low and at its extreme? We call that *tto*."

She had heard the term, so she raised her head and inhaled sharply in acknowledgment. She had never been out there at night, though. Only the following afternoon, collecting sea snails.

"We learned that fishing from ṇoniep. We go out there, and sometimes we catch a lot of *ṃōn*,[129] sometimes no. But a ṇoniep will always fill his basket with these tasty, fatty fish. He makes his hook from a fish bone or shell, and he makes his line from *arṃwe*,[130] just like we do, and he cuts his pole on the way to the ocean side just like us. So, why is he so lucky?"

She didn't bother to answer. She didn't know, and it was clear he had asked a rhetorical question.

"Well, for one thing, the ṇoniep knows everything about that small fish we call *ṃōn*. That is his pet. And another, we use the arm of a sand crab for bait, but he makes a lure from a *kōṇṇat* leaf. You know those veins on the underside of the leaf. Well, he peels them out and dries them in the sun until they turn white, and that's what he ties to his hook.

"If you keep fishing long enough, you might learn how to tell when the tide is exactly right to catch *ṃōn* and sometimes fill your basket, but he also knows the places on the reef that are best for catching these armored little red scorpions.

"So, first learn to tell when the tide is right. And then one night, you'll see him way off, but he won't be in any hurry to come up to you. First, he'll want to make sure you're not afraid of him. If you try to get up close to him, he'll keep fishing his way down the reef. So, that's not a good way to approach him. It's better to wait for him to come up to you. If you see him one night, then go ahead and fish the exact same tide the next, and you'll see him come a little closer to you this time. But don't hurry to talk. To a ṇoniep, silence is a sign of friendship. Just watch where he fishes, and now is the right time to follow him. Be silent and follow, and he'll show you all his best spots to fish.

"You'll fill your basket, but when you turn around, he'll be gone. But

[129] Bigscale soldierfish: *Myripristis berndti.*

[130] A small tree: *Pipturus argenteus* (Native mulberry); the bark ("ōr") of this tree is stripped and twisted into fishing twine.

don't worry, 'cause the next night, when the tide is right, you'll see him again and on and on. And in the morning, those people of your house will wake up and find a full basket of fish. They'll broil those fatty fish on hot rocks, and the smoke from the fat falling into the coals will fill the air with a wonderful smell, and they'll all be impressed with your fishing skill. But whatever you do, don't tell them about your friend. That is their only rule. When you make friends with a ṇoniep, you're forbidden to tell."

That was an interesting story. Helkena had heard about ṇoniep before, but not connected to *tto* fishing. The irooj was a charismatic storyteller. He had caught the attention of everyone at the *ṃōn kweiḷọk*, though he was making it clear he was telling the story to her. Even Ḷainjin managed to hold his questions, not wanting to interrupt him. The irooj was a handsome man, with his gray-streaked hair tied in a neat bun. He was young for an irooj. Most had to wait for older brothers to die before taking their turn.

He smiled at Helkena. "People of Kuwajleen tell a story of a man named Lōito. Have you heard this story?" he asked politely.

She had not and gave her head a quick twitch.

"Each morning, he would paddle west to Elij,[131] a small islet up the reef, to cut the coconut he would crush into oil for lamps and such. And each evening, he would paddle back east to Naṃ-en to sleep with his chosen woman in the village. Then one morning, he finds two old people there. Now, nobody lives on Elij, and he knows everyone on Naṃ-en, but he doesn't recognize this couple. And when he tries to approach them, they step into the brush and disappear.

"So, what is the measure of his fright? But Lōito controls himself, sits down, and starts to cut his *copra*.[132] And he thinks, 'Maybe they're a couple of ṇoniep.' And after a while, waow! He sees them again. They seem to be pulling weeds and cleaning up a bit at the edge of the brush. But he doesn't go up to them this time, and he doesn't run away. He just sits there and cuts out his copra. He thinks, 'They must be ṇoniep.'

"That evening, he paddles back to Naṃ-en, but he doesn't say anything. And next day goes the same way, only this time they get a little closer. He

---

[131] Islet of Kuwajleen (aka Kwajalein) Atoll.

[132] Dried coconut; used to make oil.

doesn't recognize them, and he's sure they're a couple of ņoniep, so he doesn't say anything to anybody. He thinks, 'If I can make friends with them, it'll be a lucky thing for me.'

"So, on and on until they start cleaning up around his house. Everything they touch somehow changes and becomes more beautiful. And their skin is so shiny and their hair too. They move very deliberately, and they smell good. But so far, that's all they do. They just clean up ... till everything begins to change.

"And then one morning, Lōito beaches his canoe and finds them cutting his copra. So, he takes his spear and walks to the ocean reef and *bbō*[133] a bit till he spears two fish. He brings them back and gives them to the old lady to cook. Then he husks several coconuts and grates them. Soon she finishes cooking and places them in a basket. They look beautiful somehow.

"So, they *jiraal*[134] together and waow! The sky of ņoniep falls upon them. When he looks out, all the brush is gone, and he sees house after house to the end of the island. He sees people as close together as the fingers of your hand. And everything under the shade of breadfruit trees... Everything has its place, neat and somehow beautiful. Men and women with long hair alike. He realizes now that the old man is an irooj.

"Lōito and the irooj walk through the village together, and everyone is peaceful and kind. Only he doesn't understand the meaning of some of the words the people speak because they use old Kajin Rālik. And everyone refers to the daughter of the irooj, but she is not around.

"On and on, every day now, when he goes to the islet, he enters the sky of ņoniep until he gets used to it. Then one day, the irooj tells Lōito he has sent word for his daughter to come from Naṃo Atoll.[135] He expects her the next day, and he wants Lōito to take her as his mate. He wants Lōito to live with them permanently. Waow! Lōito is all excited and forgets to cover up his copra. He paddles back to Naṃ-en and notices it's about to rain. He sees two men of his village paddling west, so he asks them to beach at Elij first to cover up his copra for him.

---

[133] To fish with a spear at the reef's edge.

[134] To eat grated coconut, usually with fish.

[135] Aka Namu Atoll.

"But when the men go ashore, the copra is already covered. The irooj had already covered it up. Of course, the men don't see the irooj or anything — just one old shack and the covered copra. The next morning, when they meet Lōito, they tell him about the covered copra. He doesn't say anything to them about it but paddles westward. But the men go on to speak with his chosen one, who agrees he has been strange lately.

"That day, a fleet of ņoniep canoes arrives from Naṃo. There on the first boat is the daughter of the irooj. She and Lōito take one look at each other and fall in love. They decide to start sleeping together the next night. Lōito is late to leave and darkness falls, so the irooj has two men paddle him and his canoe back to Naṃ-en.

"When they arrive, the smell of those two ņoniep scents the whole islet from one end to the other. His chosen one begins to question him. Why was his copra covered when he told the men of the islet it wasn't? Does he have another woman there or what?

"But Lōito isn't talking. He just stares off at those ņoniep and his boat beached there by the lagoon. On and on into the night she questions him. She won't let him sleep. Jealousy makes a cruel companion. Until finally, just before dawn, when he is ready to leave, he tells her he's going to live with ņoniep and won't be back.

"Waow! Right away, he knows he has made a mistake. When he goes down to his canoe, those ņoniep friends are gone. He looks all around for them, but they're gone. He paddles westward to Elij, but his old friends are gone, and they never returned to bring that sky of ņoniep again. So, what was a measure of his sadness? If you ever make friends with a ņoniep, don't tell anybody."

Helkena couldn't remember when she fell asleep that evening. She was exhausted from the voyage, and Ļainjin, as usual, slept on a mat with his favorite grandfather, Jipeba.

But the irooj awakened her with his touch on her shoulder. He held out his hand and asked her to come with him. "Of course, you don't have to come if you're tired or don't want to," he whispered. When she looked around, everyone seemed asleep. It took her only a moment to decide. She grabbed his hand, and he helped her to her feet. She was a bit disoriented.

They crossed the courtyard. "I realize I'm an old man. I can hardly get it to rise with my chosen ones anymore. I was hoping you might agree to help me. I'm sure your youth and vivacious spirit will do the trick."

She squeezed his hand more firmly to assure him she was willing.

He escorted her to the ladder beneath his house, which was strangely empty. The house was quite large, and there was only one oil lamp in a far corner. She dropped her skirts and stood naked before him.

"*Wōt jeej*!"[136] he exclaimed, slowly inspecting the tattoo embellishing her womanhood.

She stepped toward him and separated the fibers of his *in*. Touching his somewhat-erect manhood, she flashed a coquettish expression of desire that brought what she touched to immediate heed. Untying his skirt, she laid him down and plunged down onto him, hoping to harden him even more. This she accomplished, but he released his seed long before she could tickle her sensitive spot on the tip of his manhood, and the adventure ended prematurely in the usual semi-satisfied way. He escorted her back to the *m̧ōn kweiļo̧k*, where she fell asleep at once and slept till late in the morning.

After breakfast, she walked around the island, and it was a long walk indeed. There were more breadfruit trees and taro swamps here than on Nam̧dik, and more fishing canoes and proa in boathouses lining the shore. All in all, this impressive place again left her feeling inadequate, claiming an inferior atoll as home.

Their ambitious leader Japeba, having seen something unusual in the western sunset, called for their embarkment that evening after a very nice *kam̧ōļo* sponsored by his friend the *iroojļapļap*. The islanders showered the four visitors with so many gifts they nearly filled the small house where she longed to sleep, but instead, Japeba handed her the steering oar and off they sailed.

The wind held steady from the southeast, so Jipeba loosened the sheet and tightened the *tiliej* line to split the wind in their sail into two more easily managed pockets. Helkena could see from the start that, if the wind held, the return trip would be quicker than the earlier voyage. Japeba pointed to

[136] The same as "jeej." An idiom used to express surprise that translates as "heck" or "darn it."

Liṃanṃan, so low in the sky that she hid behind clouds most of the time. Still, Helkena was to keep the star well to the right of her mast as best she could. Halfway through the night, Jipeba took pity and offered to relieve her at the helm. She crawled into the little house on the outrigger platform and fell into a deep sleep at once. The last thing she remembered was the talkative boy questioning his grandfathers about something or other.

An urgent message

Helkena slept so late in the morning that Naṃdik was already in sight. So, she missed Japeba's teachings of the swell patterns south and west of it — but not the boy, who felt them much better than she did anyway. Taking the helm again, she sailed them over the western reef. There, everyone jumped off to lighten the load over the hump on the reef flat before the narrow boat channel, which people had cleared for hundreds of seasons before them.

No sooner had they walked their craft down the shore and unloaded their presents than Libwiro showed up with an urgent message from Lijitwa. Helkena was to speak with her as soon as possible. So, she gathered a few of her presents to pass on to her mentor. She left Ḷainjin in Jipeba's care, and off they trekked, down the path to the other side of the island.

She was dying to tell Libwiro about her encounter with the *iroojḷapḷap* but decided that telling the story twice would make too much of the incident. They found Lijitwa sitting in the cool breeze beneath her house, plaiting a jaki.

"How was your trip to Epoon?"

Helkena wondered how she knew she had been there. She hadn't told her. It had all happened so fast. Perhaps it had been Libwiro, or perhaps Jipeba. Anyway, it was time to blurt it out. "I had an encounter with the *iroojḷapḷap*!"

They both looked a bit stunned at that news.

"Really" was Libwiro's response.

"How was it?" asked Lijitwa.

"Disappointing, as usual. But what news do you have for me?"

"Something I think you'll find very interesting. Lerooj Argin stopped by yesterday and asked me to go with her family to Marmar tomorrow. She's holding the *keemem* for their second child there and wants me to help her prepare food. The day of *mama* that's approaching happens to coincide with the child's first birthday, so they decided, rather than split their party, to hold the *keemem* there. They've already had a new house built on the island for the occasion, and most of their rijerbal are already there. I thought you might want to take my place."

Helkena thought about the opportunity before her. What did she have to lose? "Okay."

"Waow, let me go and make the arrangements with her," said Libwiro. "If anything comes of this little game, I want it said I had played a part of it."

"Yes, that's perfect," Lijitwa said. "Tell the lerooj I sent you. Tell her I'm not feeling up to it, and tell her Helkena is much younger and stronger and will be more helpful anyway."

"Okay, I'm going down there right now," said Libwiro, and off she went.

It had all happened so fast that Helkena hardly had time to consider the consequences. For sure, Ḷōjurok had a place in the back of her mind, but she had long since thought of him as out of reach. She hadn't seen him in several seasons. Did Lijitwa know something she didn't? Helkena had fallen into a pattern of just following her advice.

Lijitwa beckoned for her to come closer and sit down. "Tell me about your encounter."

"The *iroojḷapḷap* told me this ņoniep story in his *m̧ōn kweiḷọk*. The others were there, but he made it clear he was telling the story to me. He made me feel sort of important. I fell asleep, but he came in the middle of the night to invite me to his house. He was very polite and assured me I didn't have to follow, but by then I was, you know … excited. So, I followed him. It was okay, I guess. Nothing special. Very short. He didn't get very hard, to tell you the truth. A problem he admitted to. His age, I guess. So, I tried pumping him, and he juiced me before I could give him the swirl. Can an old man like that get you pregnant?"

"Probably not. That was the right thing to do. You're not supposed to refuse an irooj. If you do bear his child, you'll be very lucky — and set for life."

"Well, I don't want to have his child. I promised myself I'd find a man here and take him home with me. Not trade the rest of my life humoring some old man, no matter how nice he is. I realize now, more than ever, I want a man I can love."

"Don't give up on Ḷōjurok. You have until the day of *mama* to show him who you are again. You and Liargin will be side by side before him. By now, she's old fish. She hasn't aged well, while you're still in your prime. Don't overlook the power of what I've taught you. It's called 'love magic.' It's that 'I can take you or leave you' attitude. I tried my best to foster that in you. It's very attractive to a man's self-centeredness. If you tend to reject him, he'll tend to follow you, if only to find out why. It's your independence that's so attractive to him. Liargin hasn't learned anything about love magic. She never asked me about it. This could be the chance you've waited so patiently for."

"Love magic? This is the first time you've spoken of that."

"Yes, but it was there in the background. It was the forest behind the trees. Remember I told you not to personalize your encounters?"

"Yes, but I wasn't sure why."

"You're used to not needing. So, when you find that one person you know you must have, you can pretend you don't and do it very convincingly. That's very powerful magic on a man who is a bit conceited and is expecting you to care for him. That 'I don't need you' attitude tends to drive him a bit crazy. It makes him do things he normally wouldn't."

"So, I'm supposed to go with them and pretend I don't want him?"

"Isn't that what you were planning to do anyway?"

"Yes, of course, so what's the difference?"

"If the time comes to choosing between you and her, keep this in mind: she is the needy one. You don't need his attention. You do not need his sex. You stand like a rock. You are independent, and that is why you are so attractive."

Then, perhaps noticing that Helkena looked tired, Lijitwa said, "Lie back, rest, and think about these things. You'll need to be at your best tomorrow."

Helkena lay back, rolled onto her side, and fell quickly asleep. She dreamed she was back on her home island, happy to be there and somehow content. When she finally awakened, it was nearly dusk and there was Libwiro.

She said, "Finally. I thought you'd never wake up. I wanted to wake you, but Lijitwa wouldn't let me. You're all set! Liargin sucked in the bait like a grouper fish. They'll be expecting you in the morning. Now, we better get going, or it'll turn dark before we get oceanside."

So, they left Lijitwa, who seemed excited that her plan was working. Hurrying along the path, they made it back before dark. Helkena was hungry, so she ate the tuna they had caught that morning raw, mixed with lime, salt, and coconut milk — with roasted breadfruit. It had become her favorite meal and provided her body with all the heat and stamina she needed, like a rock in a ground oven. She told Japeba her plan to "accompany Liargin to Marmar" the next day.

"You better leave early or be prepared for a nasty storm. We'll be along in a few days," he said.

Jipeba, playing *anidep* with Ḷainjin, had heard her plan. "Accompany Liargin or Ḷōjurok?"

This proved that Lijitwa had told him about the day Helkena had helped Ḷōjurok beach his proa and he'd responded by applying wūno to her shoulders. Lijitwa had already had this conversation with Japeba, who — not surprisingly — had kept it to himself.

She said, "Well, it's true I helped him beach his proa, and he — not Libwiro — applied the wūno to my shoulders. It's also true I thought we seemed to have eyes on each other, but that was a long time ago, and he chose Liargin. So what's more to say?"

Back in the conversation, Japeba repeated, "A man will eventually follow his throat."

At that, Helkena asked Ḷainjin if he wanted to take a trip to Marmar the next day.

"Oh yes," he said.

"Then better get a good sleep. No staying up with stories! We leave early in the morning."

She took Japeba's words of semi-encouragement to bed with her and mulled them over again and again until finally falling asleep. She awoke early the next morning with the thought that this might be her last chance to achieve the goal of bringing a man back to her home island. Despite not wanting to be overanxious, she wondered, as always, if her sister had already taken Tokki, then remembered her dream of the evening before. Everything would work out all right. "The eventualities we worry about only rarely occur," she decided, "and if they do, we find that everything worked out for the best anyway."

She woke the boy, and they ate their breakfast. Then she rolled up their jaki ko, and they headed down the path to the lagoon.

Helkena was a fast walker. With his shorter legs, Ḷainjin was practically running to keep up with her. She felt bad and slowed down. "I'm sorry. Japeba says a storm is coming so we need to hurry."

"How does he know that?"

"From the red sky."

"Doesn't a storm have black clouds?" He was nearly running again.

"I think the red is caused by something else that also causes the storm. It's not the storm itself, but something that happens before it."

"I thought red sky means calm weather?"

"That's it. The calm weather produces the storm." She realized the precocious boy had just stumbled across a connection that she was now seeing for the first time.

They stopped at Lijitwa's house. The normally windy lagoon was now as calm and smooth as swamp water. The sunrise was clear and bright red. Just what Japeba, she guessed, was expecting. It was a sign of storm.

Lijitwa seemed surprised to see the boy. "Won't he be in the way? Why don't you let him stay with me?"

Helkena looked at Ḷainjin, who remained politely quiet yet obviously wanted to accompany her. "No, I promised him Marmar. So Marmar it will be." He smiled in agreement. "We better get going."

She thanked Lijitwa for all her help then, returning to the village path, they headed south. She knew the islanders were wondering where they were going with her jaki ko, but she held her head straight and ignored their curiosity. Banana trees lined the path with such abundance that they nearly blocked the morning sun.

Arriving at Liargin's compound, they crossed the courtyard and continued to the lagoon strand, where Ḷōjurok's boat sat on the shore. No one was there. Were they to wait on the shore or turn back to the house?

While she was deciding, Ḷōjurok came walking slowly toward her, a jaki under each arm. He looked the same as he had the last time she had seen him.

"*Iọkwe.* Liargin mentioned you were coming with us. Is your life good?"

"*Ebwe,*"[137] she answered with a smile.

"Is this Ḷainjin?"

"Yes, of course."

"He has grown so much since I saw him last."

Ḷainjin beamed at him.

Ḷōjurok tied his *jaki ko* to the outrigger platform. Asking for hers, he tied it on too. "She's getting the children ready. I'll be back soon."

Ḷainjin walked down the beach and she followed, as was her habit. The red sky had faded to a wispy pink and blue. The lagoon was calm, its water sloshing with the memory of winds from days past.

"Looks like we will have to paddle to Marmar," Ḷainjin said. "I hope he lets me paddle from the bow." He ran back to Ḷōjurok's proa to check the size of his paddles and grabbed the bow paddle, which was obviously too heavy for him. "This will be fine, see?" He took a couple of digs through the air to his right and left to show her he could handle what he could barely grip.

"We'll see. Maybe the wind will pick up by the time we leave."

Ḷōjurok appeared with a basket of husked coconuts and placed it on the outrigger platform. "Here are some nuts for you to drink. She shouldn't be long now." He returned to the house.

Thirsty in the warming air, they each chose a coconut, tore off the remaining husk around the mouth, and began sucking the sweet, refreshing water.

"The ocean side seems cleaner, more open than the lagoon side. I'm glad we live over there by the ocean. Not so many people there," said Ḷainjin.

"If you lived over here, there'd be more children to play with."

---

[137] Good enough; full enough.

He thought about that for a while. “But I don’t know any of the children over here.”

“Only because you live over there.”

“It’s hot over here!”

“Not usually,” Helkena said. “It’s just there’s no wind now, and you’re wearing your kilt. You’re used to running naked and cooling yourself by the ocean.”

They passed the morning that way, talking about the sky, the lagoon, and the ocean. After a while, Ļōjurok returned and invited them to their enormous cookhouse, where their rijerbal were preparing food. “Come and have something to eat,” he said. “It looks like Liargin is causing more delay.” They waited through the rest of the morning. The rijerbal gave them *iu* heated in a jāpe with coconut milk.

On occasion, Ļōjurok would pass by on another trip to his proa. Once, he stopped and apologized for Liargin’s tardiness. “It’s one thing and then another.” The time passed until it was late afternoon.

Helkena heard Ļōjurok’s voice pleading, “Can we just go?” There was still no wind, so they couldn’t sail anyway, but she realized they had better start paddling if they were going to get there with enough time left to do anything before dark.

Liargin finally showed up, carrying one child and holding the other’s hand. She had filled out a little, as most people do as they age, and seemed to hold the same self-centered, dismissive attitude toward her rijerbal. When she forgot her fan, one of them rushed it up to her. She accepted it without a glance at the woman much less a thank you. But Helkena didn’t mind. Like she had said, Liargin was the first leroojshe had met.

Liargin gave the orders, and everybody followed. Fine. Except now the weather wasn’t looking so great. A slight breeze was blowing very softly out of the southeast, and Helkena noticed a line of clouds to the south. Ļōjurok cast them off, and they glided into the lagoon. Ļainjin scooted up to the bow, grabbed the huge oar, and helped Ļōjurok paddle lagoonward. Once they got away from shore, the line of clouds on the horizon appeared a little ominous.

“Are you sure you want to proceed?” Ļōjurok asked Liargin.

She looked at the sky with a dismissive glance. "We have to go today! We have a *keemem* to prepare! Our rijerbal are waiting for us. Those clouds look far away. The wind is blowing again, like I said it would. We'll be there long before it rains."

Ḷōjurok, of course, took the helm. After hoisting his sail in the light wind, it puffed nicely, and he headed off on a downwind reach to the north, proceeding along the shore. Liargin, distracted by her children, appeared not to notice, but Helkena was watching the line of clouds to the south rising rapidly. A line of clouds, as opposed to dark blotches of them, meant a quick change of weather, or so she had learned from Japeba. A line usually meant strong wind. Ḷōjurok was looking ahead, as was Liargin. But Ḷainjin, like Helkena, faced astern in Ḷōjurok's direction, and Ḷainjin was peering at the sky behind them.

After a while, Helkena saw Ḷōjurok glance back toward the rising cloud line and then at her. They both realized they were approaching the end of the island. This was his last chance to head shoreward, or he'd be committed to completing the trip to Marmar no matter what. If they were caught in a strong wind, it would be nearly impossible to turn around and tack back.

He turned to Liargin again. "Are you sure we shouldn't head toward shore and wait out the storm."

"Of course not!" She turned a second time to glance at the line of clouds behind them. "Those rain clouds look far away. We'll be there before it rains."

As Ḷōjurok studied Liargin, his expression was resigned. She had delayed him past all reason, and he seemed to be full of her. Like Helkena, he knew what they were probably in for. But Liargin, not used to watching the sky, had decided and so be it. And her decision would precipitate a fateful evening indeed.

He continued sailing toward Marmar. The wind began shifting southward in the direction of the threatening cloud line, and with the wind now increasing and coming directly from behind, the proa picked up speed. It soon become obvious that a storm with both wind and rain was rolling in, and it was about to catch them out on the lagoon. What had appeared in the distance as a line in the sky became an angry-looking ridge of clouds with unusual gray whisps beneath it.

A while later, these clouds began streaming above them, and the wind above suddenly fell. It swept the lagoon's surface and rushed quickly toward them.

Largin must finally have noticed the dark approaching storm because she shouted at Ḷōjurok, "Are we okay?"

He didn't get a chance to answer. The wind gushed into his full sail, and the sheet he had secured with a single loop on a peg within his reach slipped loose. He dropped his steering paddle, which was tied to his helm, and grabbed the sheet with both hands. But the pressure of the wind blowing into the belly of the full sail was too much for him to hold, and the line slid through his clenched hands, burning his fingers and cutting deep furrows into his palms. This instantly rendered his hands useless, leaving the sail to flap free in the wind nearly forward of their bow.

At the same time, a deluge of cold, horizontal raindrops stung their naked arms and backs. The children began screaming. Liargin, not understanding Ḷōjurok's predicament, cried, "Do something!" He just sat there, staring at the red meat of his bleeding palms.

Ḷainjin instinctively responded. With his paddle, he managed to fish the sheet tied to the *rojakkōrā* from the water. Then, quickly grabbing hold of the *rojakkōrā*, now behind him, with as much strength as his thin arms could muster, he turned the sail back to face the wind and then handed its sheet's end to Helkena. Without further tightening, she secured it back to its peg again.

Ḷainjin's maneuver had turned their boat to face the wind, and they were drifting rapidly northward with their *kubaak* to starboard. She realized she needed to reduce pressure on the sail before reengaging such a strong wind. Remembering how Japeba had reefed the sail returning from Kili, she stood before the mast. The rain pelted her like arrows.

She untied the *tiliej* line and hoisted it until the line parted the sail into two deep pockets. This reduced the size of the sail that would face the wind. Replacing Ḷōjurok at the helm, she sheeted in, and with their sail now properly reefed — and puffed into two pockets — she began sailing again through the wind and horizontal rain toward Marmar. She looked ahead and nodded to acknowledge Ḷainjin. He sat facing the violent rain with determination and a proud grin that showed he knew he had done well and helped to save their journey.

The other children, by contrast, were still crying. Liargin, in the interim, had unrolled a jaki and covered herself and them, their backs to the storm, as best she could. She continued to berate Ḷōjurok as though the storm was his fault, forgetting it had been her decision to continue into it. Ḷōjurok just sat silent on the outrigger platform next to them, facing Helkena and exposing his front to the biting rain. Apparently, he had resigned himself to allowing Helkena and Ḷainjin to take complete control of his boat. He just sat there, keeping his palms to himself, and let his chosen one say what she would without defending himself.

They would soon approach the island's back reef. It was filled with coral up-crops that might be dangerous, given the current tide. Helkena didn't know if it had risen enough to safely pass over them, and with the gale blowing from behind, they were sailing at incredible speed. She weaved their craft between one up-crop and then another. Given their direction, there was no way to slow the craft down.

Then Ḷainjin cried out, "Drop sail!" So, she released the sheet. The boat turned into the wind a second time, and the boy — standing on his tiptoes — released the halyard. The sail now down, she steered the craft back downwind. With its pressure again at her stern, she easily navigated the remainder of the coral heads as Ḷainjin paddled and guided between them the rest of the way to shore.

Helkena stood like a rock in the cold rain as Liargin and the children debarked and, huddling together beneath the jaki, headed toward their new house. Her rijerbal soon came to carry the proa ashore and beach it above the tide line. Then, like a man, Helkena carried the sail into the newly constructed *ṃōn kweiḷọk*. She returned to the boat to retrieve her sopping jaki.

Ḷōjurok had disappeared somewhere, so she followed Ḷainjin, who had run for the shelter of the cookhouse. Elders were sitting before a blazing fire. There, she asked Liargin's rijerbal for a *raanke* and husked coconuts, which she grated into a leaf, thinking she might as well scrub herself for the night.

A kind woman gave her directions to the bathhouse. Leaving the jaki in the *m̧ōn kweiļọk*, she roamed around in the rain until she found the thatch bathhouse. Walled and open air, it was by the well, some distance inland. She filled the *kapwōr* shell inside, placed the grated coconut into an *inpel*, and had just begun to scrub her face when she heard the stones outside the bathhouse crunch as someone softly approached.

At first, she thought it might be Ļainjin, but he never followed her to the bathhouse anymore, and the sound was too heavy. Then she wondered, "Was it him?" She peeked over the top of the thatch wall. It was him.

She could barely control herself. Her body cried out, "Take his hand and bring him inside." But she remembered Lijitwa's words and decided to play with him a bit.

"What do you want?" she asked, letting herself be seen, hanging her strong, bare arms over the bathhouse thatch. The afternoon sky was dark, and the rain, a deluge, poured straight down on them now. She held her face to the sky to rinse off the grated coconut.

Ļōjurok stood outside. His head down, he was staring at his feet like a boy caught stealing.

"You need to tell me what you want so I can help you."

"I want you."

"Then why did you choose Liargin?"

"That was a mistake. I can see that now."

"Ļōjurok, how can you undo your choice? You have two children. What about them?"

"Like all children, they'll mostly be raised by others anyway. Ultimately, there's very little for me to do. She has many rijerbal."

"No, I can't be part of this. If you want to throw away Liargin, that's your decision, but I won't be part of this now. Go away."

But she didn't turn back to her bath. She just stood there in the pouring rain. And he stood his ground on the other side of the thatch wall. Time passed.

"Here, hold out your hands," she finally said. When he did so, she squeezed coconut milk into each of his palms. "There. Now go back to your chosen one before she wonders where you are and comes looking for you."

He just stood there. She didn't turn away. After a while, he said, "I don't care if she comes and sees me begging at the bathhouse door. You asked me what I wanted. I told you."

He was like a fish at the end of her line now, and she was silently drawing him closer with every patient pull of her hands. He was the same man she had met that day on the ocean-side reef— handsome but polite and unassuming, not wordy. It reminded her of that first day long ago, when they had made friends in silence.

She prodded him to speak. "I don't know. It doesn't seem right to me."

"Is there a right or wrong when it comes to love?"

"Yes, just saying it! Love is meant to be demonstrated."

She opened the thatched bathhouse door and stood naked before him.

The sight of her very gradually brought his eyes from the ground to her between, where she wanted them. She shifted her weight to one leg and placed a hand on her hip. The other, at her side, held the *inpel* of grated coconut.

She smiled at him through the dim light and the deluge of rain. "You can see my *jukwe* now. You probably want to kiss that, don't you?"

"Yes, truly, I've never seen anything so beautiful."

"Now you're lying." She laughed. "You can hardly see it. Do you want to come in and close the door?"

Once he was inside, she gripped his shoulders tightly. "You know my time on Naṃdik is very short now."

"When I think of all the time I wasted with Liargin…"

"I was very young back then." Still gripping him, she touched his chest with her pointy breasts.

"Yes, you were a little too young and beautiful. You had me a little intimidated. I was scared of Japeba."

"Well, I've grown up now, and I've had my share of men," she admitted. She loosened her grip on him, fumbled for the drawstring of his kilt. It dropped finally, revealing his manhood, fully erect. It throbbed with pressure as she pressed her belly against it. The rain spilled down, isolating them in a world to themselves. Reaching her open mouth up to his, she darted her tongue in and out, then allowed it to swim freely, tangling with his, until their passion sank them to the coral-stone floor. There, she squatted over him and swirled her būtti around and around the sensitive tip of his manhood until her motion warmed her and her body sneezed like never before.

So fully satisfied that she had to pause, she leaned forward and they coupled their heads together for the second time. He held her close until she stopped trembling. Lifting herself up, and slowly at first, she began swirling on top of his manhood again, this time meeting his eyes with hers, each openly showing their wanton, aggressive desire for the other. This time, she rewarded his agony by plunging him deep inside — once before stimulating her sensitive spot, twice before continuing to pleasure herself, three times before achieving satisfaction a second time. Finally, she pumped him until he moaned and held tight to her, a passionate end to the storm now dwindling about them.

Happy and relieved, Helkena sat back against the thatch, his seed now planted deep inside her. Across from her, Ḷōjurok just smiled. After, they lovingly rubbed each other's bodies with coconut milk. Then they walked to the *ṃōn kweiḷọk* together.

"Where would you like to sleep?" he asked.

Thinking he was suggesting they sleep together, she knew Liargin wouldn't allow it. Then she had an even more adventurous idea. "My house?"

It took him a moment to answer. "Okay. I better say goodbye to the lerooj first."

Helkena watched him head over to the house and step up the ladder and then heard Liargin protesting loudly. He returned, walking quickly, with Liargin following.

She began shouting, accusing Helkena of bewitching her chosen one. The three of them walked through the dark and the rain to the boathouse. "Can you grab my sail?" he asked Helkena.

Helkena could barely reach it but was finally able to slide it from the rafters. She carried it down to the boat, then went to the cookhouse to retrieve Ḷainjin, leaving the couple to argue on the beach.

"Come on," she told the boy. "We have to go back home." Without complaint, he left the warmth of the fire and headed back into the lessening rain.

Suffering through Liargin's continued beratement, Ḷōjurok, with the tips of his fingers, and Helkena, with all the strength she could muster, were just able to launch the canoe. Ḷainjin, wanting to help, grabbed onto the outrigger to prevent it from dragging. Helkena took the helm, and because the wind had switched all the way around to the northeast, she and the boy were easily able to paddle them away from the beach. Liargin's shouted insults at her and final pleadings for Ḷōjurok to come to his senses became fainter with distance. They paddled through the downpour until the breeze coming around the end of the island found them. Then she raised their sail and began crossing the lagoon.

Ḷainjin, sitting again at the bow, was bearing the weather bravely, but from what little he said, she realized he had begun to shiver. And she knew a conversation was necessary. It would be awkward, so she asked him to come and sit on the outrigger platform in front of her. Ḷōjurok, already there, sat facing forward and back-to-back with him. Encouraging Ḷainjin to rest his back against Ḷōjurok's, she rubbed his small, boyish shoulders and chest with her free hand. She began in an intimate tone. They had never spoken about her personal relationships before.

"We had to get out of there. Liargin was very mad at me," she said. "Do you know why?"

"Because you're stealing her man?"

Helkena realized he knew more about her love life than he had let on. So, that part was almost over. In defense, she added, "Sometimes love makes us do bad things. You'll understand someday."

"Like when my mom left me with you because she knew a typhoon was coming and it would be risky to take me along."

"Yes. That was a bad thing, but her love for you made her do it."

"But Liargin is a lerooj. Does that make a difference?"

"I'm afraid it does. It means that the bad thing I did is even more serious. It might even affect her relationship with your grandfathers if we're not careful. Liargin may want to get even with us."

"Does it mean you have to leave us? Jipeba warned me you would be leaving soon."

"Yes, I'm afraid it does. You see, I've completed my job here. You're a grown boy now. You've already begun your training with Japeba, and you are going to grow up to be a *rijeḷā* who will sail to Wōtto and everyplace else. We'll see each other again someday. Just not here. I have to leave Naṃdik now."

He had stopped shivering. "I understand. Can I sit on the bow now?"

"Yes."

"When we get home, can I lower the halyard?"

"Yes. You did it well last time."

Ḷōjurok and Helkena were quiet for a while. He turned to face her, bonding in silence again. Then, out of the gray, he asked, "Wouldn't you think she would stop to consider that, just maybe, I might need a little adventure in my life? We were so young when we began our life together. All that time, I never considered another woman. And then suddenly, I saw the alternative. This path I never thought of taking before. This path that's more exciting and adventurous. So, I took it. Why is that so hard to understand?"

"She doesn't understand why you need adventure. She doesn't understand why she, with all her advantages, isn't enough. She's having a very bad evening right about now, and she's going to have a worse day tomorrow and the day after, when she holds her *keemem*."

"That's right. We'll be all they talk about," he said with a naughty laugh.

"Japeba says a woman always chooses the practical course of action. A man, on the other hand, follows his throat."

A while later, they beached at Lijitwa's place. What was the measure of her excitement to see the two of them together? She rushed to help them beach his proa. Everything had turned out the way she had foreseen, only more quickly than expected.

"Where to now?" Lijitwa asked, probably wondering if they needed a place to sleep that night.

Ḷōjurok looked at Helkena through the drizzle. "Wōtto?"

It was her turn to speak. She smiled and took his hand. "Wōtto it is!"

"We'll be back tomorrow," he said. "We need to walk to the ocean side and say our goodbyes to the elders."

Beside them, Ḷainjin was shivering again. Lijitwa turned to him. "Remember, you have a friend here by the lagoon."

The boy raised his head and wheezed his response.

The three of them set off on the path to the ocean side, and the rain seemed to lessen more as they walked.

Japeba and his brother were in the cookhouse. Ḷōjurok showed his palms to Japeba, who applied wūno. Then the brothers offered the couple supper, and they sat together to eat.

"So, you got caught in yesterday's storm. Why did you leave so late?" Japeba asked.

Helkena replied on Ḷōjurok's behalf. "Never mind. What's done is done, and his craft is fine."

They had prepared her favorite meal: roasted breadfruit with raw tuna marinated in lime, salt, and coconut milk. Helkena thought, "This will be the last time I will taste such wonderful food," remembering there were no limes where they were now headed.

"I jettisoned the one who made us tardy," Ḷōjurok added. "And with your permission, I'll take the one who saved the day."

"You don't need my permission," Japeba responded, staring into Ḷōjurok's eyes. "I hope you know what you're doing. It's not every day a man jilts his lerooj and his children on the day before their keemem."

"Well, I have a good excuse." Ḷōjurok offered his fingers to Helkena, who eagerly grasped them in hers.

Helkena smiled proudly at both Japeba and Ḷōjurok — and for good measure, she turned to Jipeba as well. "We leave tomorrow for Wōtto, and we've already talked about this with Ḷainjin," she said, putting her hand on his shoulder. "He agrees it's time to cut him free. He's like a grown *koon*,[138] ready to spread his wings and fly the ocean by himself now. Isn't that correct, son?"

This was the first time she had used that word to refer to him. Perhaps it brought thoughts of his true mother to all who stood there. Not willing to talk, Ḷainjin smiled his consent and bowed his head.

Exhausted, she slept on Ḷōjurok's chest. She managed to hover over him once more before the dawn, which brought a new day when all her wildest dreams came to fruition. Now hungry, they went below and found both the boy's grandfathers pleased with his reaction to their leaving. He seemed his

---

[138] Baby bird.

normal, happy self. He had passed his morning collecting broken and water-worn shells and, with Jipeba's help, drilling and stringing them together to finish a bracelet, his parting gift to her.

"Do you want us to escort you back to Wōtto?" Japeba asked.

Helkena looked to Ļōjurok, who declined. "We can follow the necklace that far."

Their plans set, the brothers set to work making *bwiro* for the voyage while Helkena delivered her parting words to the boy. He seemed to understand and didn't protest.

"I've already stayed longer than I promised my parents" was the gist of what she told him. He just put his arms around her, knowing these were their last moments. "My parents miss me as much as you miss your mother. You, too, will set off on a voyage someday, and you'll find her. I can promise you that. And you'll come and find me on Wōtto! In the meantime, keep listening to your grandfathers. They will prepare you for your search."

By noon, they had a full basket of *bwiro*, a log of *jāānkun*, and many empty netted shells for water once they reached the lagoon. After many hugs all around, Japeba gave them his parting advice. "Head east to Kili. Then, like you said, just climb the necklace — Jaluit,[139] Aelōñļapļap,[140] Naṃo, Kuwajleen, and finally Wōtto. That's easier than the way we came. More places to stop and less open ocean."

"*Jrak ilo kapin meto*!"[141] chanted Jipeba with a smile, looking at Ļainjin, assuring him she would be all right sailing to islands he had not yet seen. "We'll walk to the end of the island to see you off."

The last things Japeba gave them before they walked eastward were his fire drill and a small bundle of *bwijinbwije*.

So, Helkena and her newly chosen one turned to head down the path to the lagoon one final time. The boy clung to her waist for the last time to perhaps show it was hard to let her go, and she tied his long hair in a knot, as she was wont to do. But Jipeba ultimately led the boy away, heading north according to plan, toward the island's end.

---

[139] Atoll in the southern Rālik chain.

[140] Aka Ailinglaplap Atoll.

[141] "Sail the back side of the ocean."

They stopped so she could say goodbye to Libwiro and Libujen, who could hardly believe the rapid turn of events. Libwiro offered to accompany them but then, thankfully, remembered her parents — whom she had to look after — and perhaps the satisfying ire of the lerooj, who would likely learn everything.

When they reached the lagoon, Helkena could tell that Lijitwa's joy for her was tempered by the selfish thought that she would likely never see her again. Ļōjurok went looking for a boy to cut coconuts while the women filled the netted shells with water.

Lijitwa smiled broadly. "I take it fulfillment is no longer your problem?"

"Not even a concern. He is the one I was waiting for. Thank you for all you taught me — and for all that has occurred these last two days. It never would have happened this way without the love magic. Look at him. He's in a trance!"

Lijitwa laughed. "And by the time he wakes up, you'll be on your way to Jaluit or maybe even Aelōñļapļap! He's an honorable man. He'll stick by his commitments now that the love magic got him to choose. I predict that you'll be very happy, dear, but never stop swirling him to sleep!"

Ļōjurok returned with the coconuts. "The tide waits!"

"For no man or woman," answered Lijitwa, sharing a final, knowing glance with her protégé before she embarked.

The wind was mild and had returned to the east with the storm's passing. As Helkena and Ļōjurok crossed the reef at the island's end, there — waving their arms on the beach — were Ļainjin and his favorite grandfather. She waved frantically at the two with her braceleted arm before heading their craft across the high tide's kāleptak swells. Then they crossed the white water at the reef's edge and entered the deep-blue back side of the surrounding sea.

Interested in more of The Legends of Ḷainjin? Here's where you can purchase my other books:

Man Shark:
https://www.iguanabooks.ca/books/man-shark
The Forbidden Man:
https://www.iguanabooks.ca/books/the-forbidden-man

Reviews are important to me — especially yours! Here are the links:

Man Shark

Amazon US:
https://www.amazon.com/dp/1771802286#customerReviews
Amazon Canada:
https://www.amazon.ca/review/create-review/?ie=UTF8&channel=glance-detail&asin=1771802286
Goodreads:
https://www.goodreads.com/review/edit/48553983

The Forbidden Man

Amazon US:
https://www.amazon.com/dp/1771805080#customerReviews
Amazon Canada:
https://www.amazon.ca/review/create-review/?channel=glance-detail&asin=1771805080&ie=UTF8&
Goodreads:
https://www.goodreads.com/review/edit/59513771

Glossary

Aelōn̄ļapļap — Aka Ailinglaplap Atoll

ajet — Drift nut; sweet smelling; used with coconut oil to make perfume.

ak — The frigate bird: *Fregata magnificens.*

aļap — A paramount landholder who manages land on behalf of an irooj.

Āne-pin̄ — An islet of Aelōn̄ļapļap famous for its tattooing traditions.

anidep — A foot-sized cube of woven pandanus leaves that is kicked back and forth within a circle by clapping participants.

anjilik — Legendary sailors who live in a contemporaneous spirit world and visit on the nights before, during, and after the full moon.

añōneañ — "Call of the north"; the southern solstice, which annually coincides with winter in the northern hemisphere.

añōnrak — "Call of the south"; the northern solstice, which annually coincides with summer in the northern hemisphere.

anrā — A small tray made of coconut leaflets.

apet — The two spars that curve downward and attach the outrigger float, or "kubaak," to the underside of the outrigger platform.

arm̧we — A small tree: *Pipturus argenteus* (Native mulberry); the bark ("ōr") of this tree is stripped and twisted into fishing twine.

atat — A plant with small, thin leaves; the stems of this plant, *Triumfetta procumbens*, were processed to make skirts or kilts.

bal — The foot beneath the clew of the lateen sail where its vertical gaff and horizontal yard join.

barulep — Coconut crab.

bbō — To fish with a spear at the reef's edge.

buñtokiōñ — Swell that "falls from the north."

buñtokrear — Swell that "falls from the east."

buñtokrōk — Swell that "falls from the south."

būtti — Wart; projection from skin; slang for "clitoris."

bwebwe — Yellowfin tuna: *Neothunnus macropterus.*

bwijinbwije — A by-product of the rope-making process; densely packed strands of coconut-husk fibers too thin for rope making; used for kindling as well as washing.

bwilak — Surgeonfish: *Naso lituratus.*

bwiro — Uncooked breadfruit that has been mashed and preserved. It is somewhat odorous.

copra — Dried coconut; used to make oil.

depet āne — "Pierce islet," from the proverb "Wa jab depet āne." Literally, "boat does not pierce islet." This proverb means that a canoe's hull does not pierce the sand of an islet without bearing gifts.

Diaj — Immense coral rock on Namorik reef.

diak — To tack or, more specifically, shunt. The tack of the sail is transported from one end of the canoe to the other, keeping the outrigger to windward.

dibukae — An intermediate current surrounding an atoll.

Drej lotipen! — "They are fishing longline for tuna."

driwūno — Ones who know medicine.

Eb — Mythical cannibal isle far to the west.

Ebon — Aka Epoon. A neighboring atoll seventy-three miles south-southwest of Namorik.

ebwe — Good enough; full enough.

Elij — Islet of Kuwajleen (aka Kwajalein) Atoll.

Emejjia wa iļo̧meto! — "A boat dies slow in the open ocean."

Eneen-kio — Wake Island; traditionally, the northernmost island of the Ratak chain of the Marshall Islands.

Epoon — Aka Ebon. A neighboring atoll seventy-three miles south-southwest of Namorik.

Helkena — Ļainjin's surrogate mother.

in — Skirt or kilt made of various fibers other than grass.

inpel — The fibrous, cloth-like outer sheathing of the coconut flower buds found at the crowns of coconut trees; used to squeeze milk-like oil from coconut gratings.

iọkwe — "Aloha"; "hello (or goodbye), love."

irooj — Chief.

iroojḷapḷap — Paramount chief.

Irooj Rilik — Mythical character; Chief of the West.

iu — Often referred to as "coconut apple"; a sprouted coconut.

jāānkun — Sun-dried sheets of pandanus pulp rolled into a log and wrapped in a sheath of pandanus leaves. Taken for sustenance on long voyages.

jaki — Sleeping mat made of plaited pandanus leaves; "jaki ko" is the plural of "jaki."

Jaluit — Atoll in the southern Rālik chain.

jāpe — A wooden, trapezoid-shaped vessel carved from breadfruit wood and used as a cooking vessel or to knead breadfruit.

Japeba — Jipeba's older brother; Tarmālu's father.

Jebrọ — Aka Pleiades; constellation. Tenth-born and youngest son of Lōktañūr.

jebwatōr — Grated taro mixed with coconut milk, wrapped in taro leaves, and baked in the oven.

Jeej — An idiom used to express surprise. Translates roughly as "heck" or "darn it."

jekad — Black noddy: *Anous minutus.*

jekaro — Also called "tuba," "toddy," and various other names; the sap of the coconut palm tapped from the flower bud as it grows and continues to protrude between its mature frond leaf and the less-mature inner fronds of the palm's inner crown. The skill of making jekaro is practiced worldwide wherever palms grow.

jeḷā — A navigator's knowledge of their position at sea related to the islands that may or may not surround them.

jeḷatae — An outer current surrounding an atoll.

jepko — Mats plaited with the whole pandanus leaf.

jetmar — The night the moon rises at dusk in the island brush.

jetñōl — The night the moon rises at dusk upon the waves.

jikin bojak — A place for excretion.

Jipeba — Japeba's younger brother.

jiraal — To eat grated coconut, usually with fish.

Jirabelbel — An anjilik chief.

Jokdik — Islet of Rongelap Atoll; means "short perch."

jokkwōp — Mashed, cooked breadfruit mixed with coconut milk.

Jrak ilo kapin meto. — Sail the back side of the ocean.

juae — The innermost current surrounding an islet.

jukkwe — Sand clam; bivalve; word used to refer to one's vagina.

kabaj — Reef heron.

Kabben — The southernmost islet of Wōtto Atoll.

kabojak — To make ready; to eliminate.

Kajin Rālik — Language of the Rālik Islands, now the western chain of the Republic of the Marshall Islands.

kāleptak — Swell that "slaps from behind"; the countercurrent of the Intertropical Convergence Zone, which periodically streams through the islands just north and south of the equator.

kaṃōḷo — A newcomer celebration.

kapwōr — Giant clam: *Tridacna gigas.*

karōjep — Fishing for flying fish with coconut-shell floats.

Kārokā — Islet of Rongelap Atoll or Rongerik Atoll.

keemem — The first birthday feast after the passing of two seasons or thirteen cycles of the moon.

kiden — Soldierbush: *Tournefortia argentea.*

kilōk — A strong, trapezoid-shaped basket plaited from the central portion of a coconut leaf. It features braided handles.

kino — A fragrant, broadly lobed fern (*Phymatosorus grossus*) often used to spice earth ovens; grows at the base of trees.

kōṃkōṃ ma — To harvest breadfruit by twisting its stalk with a small stake tied diagonally to the end of a long pole.

koṃṃool — Thank you.

kōṇṇat — A short, sprawling tree that grows next to the shore; beach cabbage: *Scaevola taccada*; "naupaka" in Hawaiian.

koon — Baby bird.

kubaak — Outrigger float.

Kuwajleen — Aka Kwajalein Atoll; islets of. The largest atoll in the Rālik chain.

Kwo kenan ke etal nan lik? — "Do you want to go oceanside?"

Ḷainjin — Tarmālu's son; Japeba's grandson.

lem — A wooden scoop, sometimes attached to a handle, used to bail water from a hull or retrieve water from the ocean.

lerooj — Female chief.

Li — The female prefix; used to emphasize respect.

Libujin — Libwiro's companion.

Libwiro — Her name literally means "fermented breadfruit"; she befriends Helkena.

Lijitwa — Her name literally means "point to the boat"; Helkena's tattooist.

lik — Oceanside.

likao wūlio — Handsome young man.

Liṃanṃan — A name: "woman beautiful." "Li": the female prefix; "ṃanṃan": "very beautiful." The north star, Polaris.

Ḷō — The male prefix "Lō," when placed before a man's name, shows respect, like the female prefix, "Li."

Ḷōjurok — Argin's chosen one.

mama — To worship the anjilik spirits.

Mānnijepḷā — A mythic bird that flew passengers from one island to another.

Marmar — The northernmost islet of Namorik Atoll.

Medyeron — An islet in the northwest corner of Wōtto Atoll.

mejo — White tern: *Gygis alba.*

ṃōjọliñōr —Too much sky inside; sickness caused by sleeping under the moon too often.

ṃōlṃōl — A mackerel: *Scomber japonicus.*

ṃōn — Bigscale soldierfish: *Myripristis berndti.*

ṃōn kweiḷọk — Meeting house.

mọrojinkwōt — Aḷap rights given for bravery in battle.

Naṃdik — Aka Namorik. Where Ḷainjin lives; part of the Rālik string of islands.

Namorik — Aka Naṃdik.

Naṃo Atoll — Aka Namu Atoll.

nana — Red-footed booby: *Sula sula.*

nen — Either the fruit from *Morinda citrifolia*, a small tree prized throughout the islands for its medicinal properties, or the tree itself; a tonic thought to promote health. Also called "noni" among Polynesians.

ñi — Tattooing chisel made of albatross bone; the sharp teeth of this tool.

ņoniep — People from a spiritual world who live the old life contemporaneously with people of the present day.

or — Spiny lobster: *Panuliris penicillatus.*

pāle — Dried, braided coconut leaves used as torches for fishing; a coconut frond.

pāllep — Aka "pāllep wāto"; a specific tract of land from ocean to lagoon on Namorik Atoll.

pāllep wāto — Aka "pāllep."

pāp — The base of the coconut frond up to where the leaflets begin; coconut-leaf stems often used as rollers to slide a boat up or down the shore.

pejpetok — The spent core of a pandanus kernel drifting about in the ocean; a drifter.

pejwak — Brown noddy: *Anous stolidus.*

proa — An outrigger canoe rigged with a sail.

raanke — A stool-like apparatus shaped like a saddle with a protruding arm capped with a semi-circular shell grater.

Rālik — The western chain of atolls of what is now known as the Republic of the Marshall Islands.

rarō — Cleanup; collect fallen leaves.

rārōk — Uninhabited land.

rijeḷā — Literally, "bones that know"; traditional navigator; captain.

rijerbal — Worker; commoner.

rojak — The yard or lateral boom of the triangular lateen sail. Vertical boom: rojak ṃaan; lateral boom: rojakkōrā.

rojakkōrā —Literally, "spar woman"; the lateral boom of the triangular lateen sail.

Tarmālu — Ḷainjin's mother; Japeba's daughter.

tiliej — A reefing line running up the mast and tied midway along the sail's boom, or "rojakkōrā," to draw it closer to the vertical boom, or "rojak ṃaan."

tipñōl — Large outrigger sailing canoe, or proa.

tuar — A sweet-smelling, plant-based spice.

urōk — To fish with a line atop a canoe; slang for "intercourse."

utak — The bud sheath from which the composite coconut flower will burst. (It shoots up between a coconut frond and the tree trunk and splits open to reveal the flower buds that become coconuts. The sheath's stem eventually rots and falls off to the ground.)

wāto — A tract of land from the ocean side to the lagoon side.

wa tutu — Boat spray; windblown ocean spray.

Wōjjā — Islet of Aelōñḷapḷap Atoll.

Wōt jeej — The same as "jeej." An idiom used to express surprise that translates as "heck" or "darn it."

Wōtto — Aka Wotho Atoll. "Wotho" is the contemporary spelling.

wūno — Medicine.

wūt — Large-leafed land taro: *Alocasia macrorrhiza.*

www.ingramcontent.com/pod-product-compliance
Lightning Source LLC
Chambersburg PA
CBHW051306250626
47155CB00009B/3461
* 9 7 8 1 7 7 1 8 0 5 8 6 5 *